道林‧格雷
的畫像

The Picture of Dorian Gray

原著 _ Oscar Wilde

改寫 _ Elspeth Rawstron

譯者 _ 林育珊

ABOUT THIS BOOK

For the Student

🎧 Listen to the story and do some activities on your Audio CD.
🗩 Talk about the story.
⭐ Prepare for Cambridge English: Preliminary (PET) for schools.

For the Teacher

 A state-of-the-art interactive learning environment with 1000s of free online self-correcting activities for your chosen readers.

Go to our Readers Resource site for information on using readers and downloadable Resource Sheets, photocopiable Worksheets, and Tapescripts.
www.helblingreaders.com

For lots of great ideas on using Graded Readers consult Reading Matters, the Teacher's Guide to using Helbling Readers.

Level 4 Structures

Sequencing of future tenses	Could / was able to / managed to
Present perfect plus yet, already, just	Had to / didn't have to
First conditional	Shall / could for offers
Present and past passive	May / can / could for permission Might for future possibility
How long?	Make and let
Very / really / quite	Causative have Want / ask / tell someone to do something

Structures from lower levels are also included.

CONTENTS

Oscar Wilde was born in 1854, in Dublin, Ireland. He was a famous playwright[1], novelist, poet and wit[2]. His most famous play is *The Importance of Being Earnest*[3]. He wrote nine plays[4], but he only wrote one novel, *The Picture of Dorian Gray*. He also wrote some children's stories, *The Happy Prince and Other Tales*, but he said that they were not written for children, but for all "childlike people".

Wilde's father, Sir William Wilde, was a famous eye doctor. His mother, Jane Francesca Elgee, was a writer. At school, Wilde was very good at Greek and Latin. He won scholarships to study Classics first at Dublin College, Ireland and then later at Oxford University, England. After his graduation Wilde moved to London to live with his friend

Frank Miles, a popular portrait[5] painter. In 1881, he published[6] his first collection of poetry[7].

In 1882, Wilde sailed to New York for a lecture[8] tour of America. On his arrival, he famously said to a New York customs official[9], "I have nothing to declare[10] but my genius." He lectured on the importance of beauty in the decoration[11] of your house, in the choice of your furniture and in the clothes you wear.

In 1884, Wilde married Constance Lloyd. They had two sons. In 1887, he became the editor of a new monthly fashion magazine, *The Lady's World*. Wilde continued to write and, although many of his works shocked the Victorian society[12] of the time, they were very popular. Wilde's success, however, suffered[13] because of scandal[14] in the 1890s. In 1895 he was arrested[15] and spent two years in prison. Oscar Wilde died a poor man in 1900.

1 playwright [ˈpleˌraɪt] (n.) 劇作家
2 wit [wɪt] (n.) 機智者；幽默家
3 earnest [ˈɝnɪst] (a.) 認真的；熱心的
4 play [ple] (n.) 戲劇
5 portrait [ˈportret] (n.) 肖像
6 publish [ˈpʌblɪʃ] (v.) 出版；發行
7 poetry [ˈpoɪtrɪ] (n.) （總稱）詩
8 lecture [ˈlɛktʃɚ] (n.) 演講
9 customs official 海關官員
10 declare [dɪˈklɛr] (v.) 申報
11 decoration [ˌdɛkəˈreʃən] (n.) 裝飾
12 Victorian society 維多利亞時代的社會
13 suffer [ˈsʌfɚ] (v.) 遭受；受苦
14 scandal [ˈskændl] (n.) 醜聞
15 arrest [əˈrɛst] (v.) 逮捕

ABOUT THE BOOK

The Picture of Dorian Gray is a gothic horror[1] story (see Exercise 8, page 12), and it is the only published novel written by Oscar Wilde. When it first appeared in a monthly magazine in 1890, it was criticized[2]. Wilde then made a lot of changes to the story. The new story was published as a novel in 1891. Again, it was criticized, and it caused scandal at the time. Wilde's wife, Constance said, "Since Oscar wrote *Dorian Gray* no one will speak to us." W.H. Smiths, the famous bookseller[3], refused[4] to sell the book, but despite[5] the controversy[6], it was still very popular.

Oscar Wilde was a successful playwright and *The Picture of Dorian Gray* is written more in the style of a play than a

novel. There is more dialogue than description and the novel focuses on the witty[7] conversations between its three main characters[8]: Basil Hallward, the artist, Lord Henry Wotton, his wealthy[9] friend, and Dorian Gray, a handsome young man.

One of the main themes[10] of the novel is the emptiness[11] of worshipping[12] beauty and pleasure. Life, Lord Henry Wotton says in the novel, should be lived for beauty and pleasure and not for duty[13]. He encourages Dorian Gray to enjoy himself. He tells Dorian he should make the most of his youth and beauty before they fade[14]. Dorian Gray takes his advice and leads a selfish, hedonistic[15] life. In the end, he realizes his mistake but it is too late. He has destroyed[16] his soul.

The novel has always been very popular and thirteen film versions of it have been made to date[17]. Marvel Comics made an illustrated adaptation[18] of the novel in 2007.

---

1 gothic horror 哥德式恐怖小說
2 criticize [ˈkrɪtɪˌsaɪz] (v.) 批評
3 bookseller [ˈbʊkˌsɛlɚ] (n.) 書商
4 refuse [rɪˈfjuz] (v.) 拒絕
5 despite [dɪˈspaɪt] (prep.) 儘管
6 controversy [ˈkɑntrəˌvɝsɪ] (n.) 爭議
7 witty [ˈwɪtɪ] (a.) 機智的
8 character [ˈkærɪktɚ] (n.) 角色
9 wealthy [ˈwɛlθɪ] (a.) 富有的
10 theme [θim] (n.) 主題

11 emptiness [ˈɛmptɪnɪs] (n.) 空虛
12 worship [ˈwɝʃɪp] (v.) 崇拜
13 duty [ˈdjutɪ] (n.) 義務；責任
14 fade [fed] (v.) 凋謝；枯萎；褪色
15 hedonistic [ˌhidəˈnɪstɪk] (a.) 快樂主義者的
16 destroy [dɪˈstrɔɪ] (v.) 毀滅
17 to date 迄今
18 adaptation [ˌædæpˈteʃən] (n.) 適應；改編

1 Match the words from the novel to the pictures.

- a) frame
- b) sitter
- c) portrait
- d) artist
- e) brushes
- f) easel

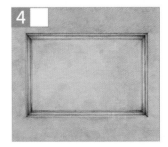

2 Label the picture with the theater words.

a actor

b stage

c actress

d audience

3 Have you ever been to the theater? Tell a friend.

4 Match the descriptions to the pictures of the characters.

a) Dorian Gray is a very good-looking young man. He has got blond hair and blue eyes.

b) Basil Hallward is an artist. He paints a portrait of Dorian Gray. He has got black hair and a strong face.

c) Lord Henry Wotton has got brown hair and a pointed beard. He always dresses very well, and he is interested in art. He has a big influence on Dorian Gray.

d) Sibyl Vane is a very beautiful young actress. She has got long dark hair and blue eyes. She is very talented.

e) James Vane is Sibyl's younger brother. He is big and tall and he wears rough clothes. He is not good-looking.

f) Alan Campbell has got dark hair. He is Dorian Gray's friend. He is a scientist.

5 Match the verbs with their synonyms.

_____	a leap	1	talk very quietly
_____	b swear	2	understand the value of
_____	c weep	3	look at for a long time
_____	d whisper	4	jump
_____	e stare	5	hit
_____	f destroy	6	cry
_____	g hurry	7	promise
_____	h strike	8	kill
_____	i appreciate	9	go quickly
_____	j murder	10	ruin

6 Complete the statements from the novel with the words below. Then check your answers on the page numbers given.

tired   laughter   disappointed   youth   curious   mysterious

a I love secrecy. It's the one thing that can make modern life
_____. (Page 16)

b _____ is a good beginning for a friendship,
and it's the best ending for one. (Page 18)

c _____ is the one thing worth having. (Page 24)

d Men marry because they're _____. Women
marry because they're _____. Both are
_____. (Page 30)

7 Do you agree with any of these statements? Tell a friend.

8 *The Picture of Dorian Gray* is described as a gothic horror story. What do you think this means? Tick (✓).

_____ a) A story about investigating and solving crimes.

_____ b) A story combining elements of horror with romance.

_____ c) A story about science and technology of the future.

9 Look at the pictures in the book. What do you think happens in the story? Tick (✓). There will be . . .

☐ a death   ☐ a marriage   ☐ a murder

☐ a war   ☐ a romance   ☐ a birth

10 Read the following extracts from the story.
What do they have elements of? Tick (✓).

a

"Oh, Henry! Every night, I go to see her act, and every night she is more wonderful."

☐ horror
☐ comedy
☐ ghost
☐ science
☐ romance
☐ technology

b

After a little while, a black shadow moved out into the light and came close to him. He felt a hand on his arm, and he looked round. It was one of the women from the bar. "Why didn't you kill him? You fool! He has lots of money, and he's bad."

☐ horror
☐ comedy
☐ ghost
☐ science
☐ romance
☐ technology

A lovely scent[1] of flowers filled the studio[2]. The light summer wind blew through the trees in the garden, and in through the open door. Lord Henry Wotton was lying on a divan[3].

In the center of the room, there was a portrait of a very beautiful young man. In front of it, sat the artist, Basil Hallward.

"It's your best work, Basil," said Lord Henry. "You must send it to a gallery[4]."

"I won't send it anywhere," Basil answered.

Lord Henry looked at him in surprise. "Not send it anywhere? My dear fellow[5], why?"

"I know you'll laugh at me," Basil replied, "but I can't exhibit[6] it. There is too much of *me* in it."

Lord Henry laughed. "Too much of *you* in it! The portrait doesn't look like you at all. You have a strong face and coal-black[7] hair. This young man is made out of ivory[8] and rose petals[9]. He never thinks. I'm sure of that. He's some brainless[10] beautiful boy. You aren't like him at all."

"You don't understand me, Henry," answered Basil. "Of course, I don't look like Dorian Gray."

---

1 scent [sɛnt] (n.) 氣味；香味
2 studio [ˋstjudɪˌo] (n.) 工作室
3 divan [dɪˋvæn] (n.)
   長沙發椅
4 gallery [ˋgælərɪ] (n.) 畫廊；美術館

5 fellow [ˋfɛlo] (n.) 傢伙；同伴
6 exhibit [ɪgˋzɪbɪt] (v.) 展示
7 coal-black [ˋkolˌblæk] (a.) 黑如煤炭的
8 ivory [ˋaɪvərɪ] (n.) 象牙
9 petal [ˋpɛtl] (n.) 花瓣
10 brainless [ˋbrenlɪs] (a.) 沒有大腦的
   （形容笨的）

"Dorian Gray? Is that his name?" asked Lord Henry.

"Yes, that's his name. I didn't want to tell you."

"But why not?"

"Oh, I can't explain. When I like people, I never tell their names to anyone. I love secrecy. It's the one thing that can make modern life mysterious[1]. I suppose you think I'm foolish."

Lord Henry laughed and pulled out his watch. "I must go, Basil," he said. "But before I go, you must answer my question."

"What is that?" asked Basil.

"Why won't you exhibit Dorian Gray's picture? I want the real reason."

---

1 mysterious [mɪsˈtɪrɪəs] (a.) 神祕的
2 sitter [ˈsɪtɚ] (n.) 肖像模特兒

"Every portrait that is painted with feeling is a portrait of the artist, not of the sitter[2]. I don't want to exhibit this picture because it shows the secret of my soul."

Lord Henry laughed. "And what is that?" he asked.

"Two months ago, I went to a party at Lady Brandon's. After about ten minutes, while I was talking to overdressed[3] ladies and boring academics[4], I suddenly felt that someone was looking at me. I turned, and I saw Dorian Gray for the first time. When our eyes met, I went pale. I felt that there was about to be a terrible crisis[5] in my life.

---

3 overdressed [ˈovəˌdrɛst] (a.) 過度打扮的
4 academic [ˌækəˈdɛmɪk] (n.) 大學教授
5 crisis [ˈkraɪsɪs] (n.) 危機

"I was afraid, and I turned to leave the room. I walked quickly to the door. But, I bumped into[1] Lady Brandon, who pulled me back into the party and I found myself face to face with the young man. I asked Lady Brandon to introduce me to him."

"And how did Lady Brandon describe this wonderful young man?" asked Lord Henry.

"Oh, something like this. 'Charming[2] boy—I forget what he does—maybe he doesn't do anything—oh, yes, he plays the piano—or is it the violin, dear Mr Gray?' We both laughed, and we became friends at once."

"Laughter is a good beginning for a friendship, and it's the best ending for one," said Lord Henry.

"Tell me more about Mr Dorian Gray, Basil. How often do you see him?" continued Lord Henry.

"Every day. I need to see him every day."

"But I thought you only cared about your art."

"He is my art to me now," said Basil. "The work I've done, since I met Dorian Gray, is the best work of my life."

"Basil, this is extraordinary[3]! I must see Dorian Gray."

Basil got up from the chair he was sitting on, and he walked up and down the room. He thought for a while and then he said, "Henry, Dorian Gray gives me inspiration[4]. But you might see nothing in him."

"Then why won't you exhibit his portrait?" asked Lord Henry.

"I don't want to show my soul to the world."

"Poets are not like you. Poets know a broken heart sells many books."

"I hate them for it," cried Basil. "An artist should create beautiful things, but he shouldn't put anything of his own life into them. Nowadays[5] men use art as a form of autobiography[6]. We have lost the abstract[7] sense of beauty. That's why the world will never see my portrait of Dorian Gray."

Art

- What do YOU think? Should art be autobiographical or just beautiful?
- Can you think of or find any examples of autobiographical art? Discuss in groups.

"I think you're wrong, Basil," said Lord Henry. Then he added, "My dear fellow, I've just remembered."

"Remembered what, Henry?"

"Where I heard the name, Dorian Gray."

"Where was it?" asked Basil, with a frown[8].

---

1 bump into 撞見
2 charming [`tʃɑrmɪŋ] (a.) 有魅力的
3 extraordinary [ɪk`strɔrdn͵ɛrɪ] (a.) 非凡的
4 inspiration [͵ɪnspə`reʃən] (n.) 靈感

5 nowadays [`nauə͵dez] (adv.) 時下；當今
6 autobiography [͵ɔtəbaɪ`ɑgrəfɪ] (n.) 自傳
7 abstract [`æbstrækt] (a.) 抽象的
8 frown [fraun] (n.) 皺眉；蹙額

"Don't look so angry, Basil. It was at my aunt, Lady Agatha's house. She told me about a wonderful young man. He's helping her in the East End[1], and his name's Dorian Gray. She said that he was very serious and kind."

"I don't want you to meet him, Henry."

Just then, the butler[2] came in.

"Mr Dorian Gray is in the hall, Sir," he said.

"You must introduce me now," cried Lord Henry, laughing.

Basil looked at Lord Henry. "Dorian Gray is my dearest friend," he said. "Your aunt was right about him. Don't spoil[3] him. Don't try to influence[4] him. Your influence will be bad."

"Nonsense[5]!" said Lord Henry, smiling. "Show him in," he added to the butler.

Bad influence

- Do you think people or friends can have a good or bad influence on each other? How? Discuss with a partner.

---

1 East End 倫敦東區（在當時代 是倫敦較貧窮的區域）
2 butler [ˋbʌtlɚ] (n.) 男管家
3 spoil [spɔɪl] (v.) 帶壞（某人）（三態： spoil; spoiled, spoilt; spoiled, spoilt）
4 influence [ˋɪnfluəns] (v.) 影響
5 nonsense [ˋnɑnsɛns] (int.) 胡說

"Basil, I'm tired of sitting, and I don't want a life-sized[6] portrait of myself," said a voice from outside the open door.

Then Dorian Gray walked into the room. When he saw Lord Henry, he was embarrassed[7]. "I'm sorry, Basil. I didn't know you had a visitor with you."

"This is Lord Henry Wotton, Dorian, a friend of mine," Basil said.

"It's a pleasure to meet you," said Lord Henry. "My Aunt Agatha has often spoken to me about you. You're one of her favorites."

"I'm in Lady Agatha's black books[8] at present," answered Dorian. "I promised to go to a club in Whitechapel with her last Tuesday, and I forgot all about it. She wanted me to play a duet[9] with her on the piano."

"I don't think it really matters[10] that you weren't there. The audience[11] probably thought it was a duet. When Aunt Agatha plays the piano, she makes enough noise for two people," said Lord Henry.

"That's very horrid[12] of you," answered Dorian, laughing.

---

6 life-sized [ˈlaɪfˌsaɪzd] (a.) 與實物大小一樣的

7 embarrassed [ɪmˈbærəst] (a.) 尷尬的

8 in someone's black books 被列入某人的黑名單（表示不受某人歡迎）

9 duet [duˈɛt] (n.) 二重唱

10 matter [ˈmætɚ] (v.) 有關係

11 audience [ˈɔdɪəns] (n.) 觀眾

12 horrid [ˈhɔrɪd] (a.) 可怕的

Lord Henry looked at him. Yes, he was handsome, with his scarlet[1] lips, his blue eyes, and his golden hair.

Basil mixed his colors and got his brushes[2] ready. He looked worried.

"Henry," he said. "I want to finish this picture today. Can I ask you to leave?"

Lord Henry smiled and looked at Dorian Gray. "Shall I go, Mr Gray?" he asked.

"Oh, please don't."

"Very well, I'll stay. You don't really mind, Basil, do you? You like your sitters to have someone to chat to."

"If Dorian wishes it, of course you must stay," said Basil.

"And now, Dorian, get up on the platform[3]. Don't listen to Lord Henry. He's a very bad influence on all his friends, except for me[4]."

Basil painted and Lord Henry chatted to Dorian. "Basil, I'm tired of standing," cried Dorian Gray suddenly. "I must go and sit in the garden. The air is too hot in here."

"I'll go out to the garden with you," said Lord Henry.

"Don't keep Dorian too long. I want to finish the painting. It's going to be my masterpiece[5]."

Lord Henry went out to the garden with Dorian. "Let's sit in the shade," said Lord Henry. "You mustn't get sunburned[6]."

1 scarlet [ˈskɑrlɪt] (a.) 緋紅色
2 brush [brʌʃ] (n.) 筆刷
3 platform [ˈplæt͵fɔrm] (n.) 臺子
4 except for sb 除了某人之外
5 masterpiece [ˈmæstɚ͵pis] (n.) 傑作
6 sunburned [ˈsʌnbɝnd] (a.) 曬黑的

🎧 10

"That doesn't matter," cried Dorian Gray, laughing.

"It should matter, Mr Gray."

"Why?"

"Because you're young, and youth is the one thing worth having."

"I don't feel that, Lord Henry."

"No, you don't feel it now. One day, when you're old and wrinkled[1] and ugly, you'll feel it. You smile? When you've lost your youth, you won't smile. When your youth goes, your beauty will go with it. Enjoy your youth while you have it. Don't waste your golden days helping the sick and the poor. Live! Flowers die, and they blossom[2] again. But we never get back our youth."

Youth

- Write down five things about youth. They can be positive[3] or negative[4]. Show them to a friend.

Suddenly Basil appeared at the door of the studio. "I'm waiting," he cried. "Please come in. The light is perfect."

---

1 wrinkled ['rɪŋkld] (a.) 有皺紋的
2 blossom ['blɑsəm] (v.) 開花
3 positive ['pɑzətɪv] (a.) 正面的
4 negative ['nɛgətɪv] (a.) 負面的

They walked down the path together. "Are you glad[1] you've met me, Mr Gray?" said Lord Henry, looking at him.

"Yes, I'm glad now. But shall I always be glad?"

"Always! That's a terrible word. Women are very fond of[2] it. They spoil every romance[3] by trying to make it last forever."

They entered the studio, and Dorian Gray stepped up on the platform again. Lord Henry sat down in a large armchair and watched him.

After about quarter of an hour, Basil stopped painting. "It's finished," he cried.

Then he wrote his name in long red letters on the left-hand[4] corner of the canvas[5].

Dorian looked at his portrait, and he realized for the first time that he was very good-looking[6]. "I understand Lord Henry's words now. Yes, there will be a day when my face will be wrinkled and I'll be old and ugly." As he thought this, a sharp pain struck[7] him like a knife.

"Don't you like it?" cried Basil.

"Of course he likes it," said Lord Henry. "It's wonderful. Sell it to me."

"It's not mine, Henry."

"Whose is it?"

"Dorian's, of course," answered Basil.

1 glad [glæd] (a.) 高興的
2 be fond of 喜歡
3 romance [ro`mæns] (n.) 戀愛
4 left-hand [`lɛft`hænd] (a.) 左側的
5 canvas [`kænvəs] (n.) 帆布；油畫布
6 good-looking [`gʊd`lʊkɪŋ] (a.) 長相好看的
7 strike [straɪk] (v.) 打；擊（三態：strike; struck; struck, stricken）

"He's a very lucky man," said Lord Henry.

"How sad it is!" said Dorian Gray. "I'll grow old and ugly. But this portrait will always stay young. It will never be older than it is today. I wish it were the other way round! I wish I could always be young, and the portrait could grow old! I would give my soul for that. Lord Henry Wotton is right. Youth is the only thing worth having. When I see that I'm growing old, I shall kill myself."

Basil turned pale[8]. "Dorian!" he cried. "Don't talk like that."

"What do you care, Basil? Your art is more important to you than your friends. I'm jealous[9] of the painting. Oh, why did you paint it?" asked Dorian.

Wish

- What does Dorian wish for? Write it down.

"This is your fault[10], Henry," said Basil angrily. "I won't let this painting spoil our friendship."

Dorian watched Basil as he walked to a table by the window. He was looking for the palette knife[11]. He found it.

---

8 pale [pel] (a.) 蒼白的
9 jealous ['dʒɛləs] (a.) 妒忌的；吃醋的
10 fault [fɔlt] (n.) 過錯
11 palette knife 調色刀

13   "He's going to tear[1] the canvas," thought Dorian. He ran over to Basil. He took the knife out of Basil's hand, and he threw it across the studio. "Don't, Basil!" he cried. "It's murder!"

"I'm glad you appreciate[2] my work at last, Dorian," said Basil.

"I love it, Basil. It's part of me."

"Well, as soon as you're dry, I'll frame[3] you, and send you home. Then you can do what you like with yourself." There was a knock at the door, and the butler entered with the tea.

"Let's go to the theater tonight," said Lord Henry.

"I'd like to come to the theater with you, Lord Henry," said Dorian.

"What about you, Basil?"

"I can't. I've got a lot of work to do."

"Well, then, you and I will go alone, Mr Gray."

"I'd like that," said Dorian.

Basil frowned and walked over to the portrait. "I'll stay with the real Dorian," he said, sadly.

"Is it the real Dorian?" cried the young man. "Am I really like that?"

"Yes, you are just like that," said Basil.

"How wonderful, Basil!"

"At least you are like the portrait in appearance[4]. The portrait will never change," sighed Basil. "That is something."

---

1 tear [tɛr] (v.) 撕破 (三態：tear; tore; torn)
2 appreciate [əˈpriʃɪˌet] (v.) 欣賞
3 frame [frem] (v.) 裱框
4 appearance [əˈpɪrəns] (n.) 外貌

Chapter 3

One afternoon, a month later, Dorian Gray was sitting in an armchair, in the little library of Lord Henry's house in Mayfair[1].

"Never marry," said Lord Henry. "Men marry because they're tired. Women marry because they're curious. Both are disappointed."

"I don't think I'll marry, Henry. I'm too much in love."

"Who are you in love with?" said Lord Henry.

"With an actress," said Dorian Gray. "Her name is Sibyl Vane."

"I've never heard of her."

"No one has. People will one day, however. She's wonderful."

"How long have you known her?"

"About three weeks."

"And where did you meet her?"

"Well, one evening, I decided to go out in search of some adventure. I found a strange little theater and decided to go in. The play was *Romeo and Juliet*. It was a dreadful[2] place, but I decided to watch the first act. Romeo was a stout[3] elderly[4] gentleman. Mercutio was almost as bad. But Juliet! She was the loveliest girl I've ever seen in my life. She's about seventeen years old, and she's got a little flowerlike face, wavy[5] dark hair, violet eyes and lips like the petals of a rose. And her voice—I've never heard such a beautiful voice . . ." Dorian paused.

"Henry, I love her," he continued. "Night after night, I go to see her act. Actresses are wonderful; actresses are different!"

"Henry!" said Dorian. "Why didn't you tell me that the only thing worth loving is an actress?"

"Because I've loved so many of them, Dorian," Lord Henry replied.

"Now I regret[6] telling you about Sibyl Vane."

"You had to tell me, Dorian. All through your life, you'll tell me everything you do."

"Yes, that's true. You have a strange influence over me. If I ever commit a crime[7], I'll come and tell you."

"People like you don't commit crimes, Dorian. And now tell me: have you met her?"

"Of course. I met her on the third night. She was playing Rosalind. I threw her some flowers, and she looked at me. That night, an old man offered to take me backstage[8], so I went. We were both very nervous. The old man kept calling me 'My Lord,' so I told Sibyl that I was not a lord. She said, 'You look more like a prince. I'll call you Prince Charming[9]' Oh, Henry! Every night, I go to see her act, and every night she is more wonderful."

---

1 Mayfair ['mefɛr] (n.) 梅費爾區
  （倫敦上流住宅區）
2 dreadful ['drɛdfəl] (a.) 糟透的
3 stout [staʊt] (a.) 矮胖的
4 elderly ['ɛldəlɪ] (a.) 上了年紀的
5 wavy ['wevɪ] (a.) 波浪的

6 regret [rɪ'grɛt] (v.) 後悔
7 crime [kraɪm] (n.) 犯罪
8 backstage ['bæk'stædʒ] (n.) 後臺
9 Prince Charming 白馬王子
  （灰姑娘童話中的王子）

"So that's why you never dine[1] with me now. I thought you must be in love. You can dine with me tonight, Dorian, can't you?"

He shook[2] his head.

"Henry, I want you and Basil to come and see her act. I know you'll both love her. Then we must get her out of that theater. She has to work for the old man for three years. So, I shall have to pay him something, of course. When all that is settled[3], I shall take a West End[4] theater for her. She'll make the world as mad[5] as she has made me."

"That's not possible, my dear boy."

"Yes, it is."

"Well, when shall we go?" asked Lord Henry.

"Let's go tomorrow," Dorian replied. "She plays[6] Juliet tomorrow."

"All right. Will you tell Basil or shall I write to him?"

"Dear Basil! I haven't seen him for a week. It's very bad of me. He sent me my portrait in a wonderful frame. I'm a little jealous of the picture because it's a month younger than I am, but I love it. Perhaps you should write to him. I don't want to see him alone. He says things that annoy[7] me. He gives me good advice."

---

1 dine [daɪn] (v.) 用餐
2 shake [ʃek] (v.) 搖動（三態：shake; shook; shaken）
3 settle [ˈsɛtl] (v.) 安頓
4 West End 倫敦西區（倫敦的時尚流行區，大型劇院林立）
5 mad [mæd] (a.) 瘋狂的；著迷的
6 play [ple] (v.) 扮演
7 annoy [əˈnɔɪ] (v.) 惹惱

Basil

- Why is Dorian not such good friends with Basil any more?
- Why does Basil annoy Dorian?

Dorian Gray put some perfume[1] on his handkerchief. "And now I must go," he said. "Don't forget about tomorrow. Goodbye."

That night, when Lord Henry arrived home, at about half-past twelve, he saw a telegram[2] on the hall table. It was from Dorian Gray. It said, "I'm engaged to[3] be married to Sibyl Vane."

TELEGRAPH COMPANY

To: Lord Henry Wotton
From: Dorian Gray

I'm engaged to be married
to Sibyl Vane.

Chapter 4

"Mother, I'm so happy!" whispered[4] the girl. "And you must be happy, too!"

Mrs Vane looked sad. "Happy!" she repeated, "I'm only happy, Sibyl, when I see you act. You mustn't think of anything but your acting. Mr Isaacs has been very good to us, and we owe[5] him money."

"Money, Mother?" the girl cried. "What does money matter? Love is more important than money."

"Mr Isaacs has given us fifty pounds to pay off[6] our debts[7]. You mustn't forget that, Sibyl. Fifty pounds is a lot of money. Mr Isaacs is very kind."

"We don't need him any more, Mother," said Sibyl. "We've got Prince Charming now." Then she paused[8]. "I love him," she said.

"Foolish child!" said her mother. The girl laughed again.

Then her mother said, "This young man might be rich. If he is rich, you should marry him. But you're too young to fall in love[9]. Besides[10], you don't know anything about him. You don't even know his name. I'm worried. And I'm upset[11] because your brother is going away to Australia."

---

1 perfume [ˈpɝfjum] (n.) 香水
2 telegram [ˈtɛləˌɡræm] (n.) 電報
3 be engaged to 訂婚
4 whisper [ˈhwɪspɚ] (v.) 低聲說
5 owe [o] (v.) 欠債
6 pay off 償清債務

7 debt [dɛt] (n.) 債
8 pause [pɔz] (v.) 暫停
9 fall in love 戀愛
10 besides [bɪˈsaɪdz] (adv.) 此外
11 upset [ʌpˈsɛt] (a.) 心煩的

At that moment, the door opened and a young man with brown hair came into the room. James Vane was big, and his hands and feet were large and clumsy[1]. He was not as genteel[2] as his sister. Mrs Vane looked at him and smiled.

"Ah, James," Sibyl cried. And she ran across the room and hugged him.

James Vane looked into his sister's face with affection[3]. "Come for a walk with me, Sibyl. I don't think I'll ever see this horrid London again."

"My son, don't say that," said Mrs Vane. "When you've made your fortune[4], you'll leave Australia and come back to London."

"I'd like to make some money to take you and Sibyl off the stage[5]. I hate it."

"Oh, James!" said Sibyl, laughing. "How unkind of you! But do you really want to go for a walk with me? Let's go to the park."

"Very well," he said, "but don't be a long time dressing[6]."

Sibyl danced out of the door. He could hear her singing as she ran upstairs. He walked up and down the room two or three times. Then he turned to his mother. "Are my things ready?" he asked.

"Yes, James," she answered. "I hope you'll be happy, James, with life at sea[7]."

---

1 clumsy [ˈklʌmzɪ] (a.) 笨拙的
2 genteel [dʒɛnˈtil] (a.) 文雅的；有教養的
3 affection [əˈfɛkʃən] (n.) 鍾愛
4 make one's fortune 發財
5 stage [stedʒ] (n.) 舞臺
6 dress [drɛs] (v.) 穿著
7 at sea 在海上；在航海中

"I hear a gentleman comes every night to the theater and goes backstage to talk to Sibyl. Is that right?" asked James.

"In the acting profession[1], we receive a lot of attention. I used to receive lots of flowers at one time. As for Sibyl's young man, he's a perfect gentleman. He's always polite[2] to me, and the flowers he sends are lovely."

"You don't know his name, though," said James angrily.

"No," answered his mother. "He hasn't told us his real name. I think it's very romantic of him. He's probably an aristocrat[3]."

James Vane frowned. "Please, look after Sibyl, Mother," he cried.

"I always look after Sibyl. This gentleman might be wealthy. It might be a brilliant[4] marriage for Sibyl."

Then the door opened and Sibyl ran in. "You're both very serious!" she cried. "What's the matter?"

"Nothing," James answered. "We must be serious sometimes. Mother, everything is packed[5], I'll be back later to say goodbye properly[6]."

"Let's go, Sibyl," said her brother impatiently[7].

They went out and walked along the dreary[8] Euston Road. Sibyl chatted about the ship and James's new life in Australia.

James listened to her. He was worried about leaving home, and most of all about leaving Sibyl. She needed protecting[9]. This Prince Charming meant her no good[10]. His mother was shallow[11] and vain[12]. She couldn't protect Sibyl. Also there was something he wanted to ask his mother. He heard someone whispering a comment about her one night at the theater. He frowned.

The Picture of Dorian Gray

"You're not really listening to me, James," cried Sibyl, "and I'm making the most wonderful plans for your future. Please say something."

"You have a new friend, I hear. Who is he? Why haven't you told me about him? He means you no good."

"Stop, James!" she exclaimed[13]. "You mustn't say anything against him. I love him."

"But you don't even know his name," answered James. "Who is he? I want to know."

"He's called Prince Charming. One day you'll meet him—when you come back from Australia. And I know you'll like him. Everybody likes him, and I . . . love him. I wish you could come to the theater tonight. He's coming, and I'm going to play Juliet. Imagine, James, to be in love and play Juliet!"

"He's a gentleman," said James.

"A prince!" she cried. "What more do you want?"

"I want you to beware of[14] him."

"To see him is to worship him."

"Sibyl, you're mad about him."

---

1 profession [prəˋfɛʃən] (n.) 職業
2 polite [pəˋlaɪt] (a.) 禮貌的；斯文的
3 aristocrat [æˋrɪstəˌkræt] (n.) 貴族
4 brilliant [ˋbrɪljənt] (a.) 耀眼的
5 pack [pæk] (v.) 打包
6 properly [ˋprɑpəlɪ] (adv.) 適當地
7 impatiently [ɪmˋpeʃəntlɪ] (adv.) 沒耐性地
8 dreary [ˋdrɪərɪ] (a.) 陰鬱的
9 protect [prəˋtɛkt] (v.) 保護
10 mean sb no good 對某人心懷不軌
11 shallow [ˋʃælo] (a.) 膚淺的
12 vain [ven] (a.) 愛慕虛榮的
13 exclaim [ɪksˋklem] (v.) 叫喊著說出
14 beware of sb 提防某人

She laughed and took his arm. "Be happy for me. Life's been hard for us both. But it will be different now. You're going to a new world, and I've found one."

"If he hurts you, I'll kill him," said James.

Sibyl looked at him in horror. He repeated his words. They cut the air like a dagger[1]. People stared at them.

"Let's go, James," Sibyl whispered.

He followed her as she walked through the crowd.

At Marble Arch, they got on a bus, which took them close to their simple home on the Euston Road.

It was after five o'clock, and Sibyl had to lie down for a couple of hours before acting. She said goodbye to her brother. There were tears in his eyes as he went downstairs.

His mother was waiting for him as he came downstairs. Their eyes met.

"Mother, I want to ask you something before I leave," he said. "Tell me the truth. Were you married to my father?"

Mrs Vane knew that she had to answer this question. "No," she answered.

"My father was a scoundrel[2] then!" cried James.

1 dagger [ˋdægɚ] (n.) 短劍；匕首
2 scoundrel [ˋskaʊndrəl] (n.) 無賴

She shook her head. "I knew he was married. We loved each other very much. If he was alive now, he'd look after[1] us. Don't speak badly of him, my son. He was your father, and a gentleman."

James was angry. "It's a gentleman who is in love with Sibyl, isn't it?"

His mother wiped[2] her eyes with shaking hands. "Sibyl has a mother," she said. "I had none."

James was touched[3]. He went over to her, and he bent down to kiss her. "I'm sorry," he said. "I must go now. But believe me, if this man does anything to hurt my sister, I'll find him and kill him. I swear[4] it."

Then James had to leave for the ship. His mother waved[5] from the window, as he walked away.

Protective

- Do you think James is right to be protective of his sister?
- Do you have a brother, sister or friend you are protective of? Tell a friend.

1 look after 照顧
2 wipe [waɪp] (v.) 擦拭
3 touched [tʌtʃt] (a.) 受感動的
4 swear [swɛr] (v.) 發誓（三態：swear; swore; sworn）
5 wave [wev] (v.) 揮手
6 suppose [sə'poz] (v.) 猜想
7 position [pə'zɪʃən] (n.) 地位

8 approve [ə'pruv] (v.) 贊成；同意
9 champion ['tʃæmpɪən] (n.) 擁護者
10 passionately ['pæʃənɪtlɪ] (adv.) 熱烈的
11 adore [ə'dor] (v.) 愛慕
12 fascinated ['fæsn,etɪd] (a.) 著迷的
13 You don't mean that.
   你不是真的這樣想。

Chapter 5

"I suppose[6] you've heard the news, Basil?" said Lord Henry that evening at dinner.

"No, Henry," answered Basil. "What is it?"

"Dorian Gray is engaged to be married," said Lord Henry.

Basil frowned. "Impossible!"

"It's true."

"To whom?"

"To a little actress."

"But think of Dorian's position[7], and wealth. He can't marry an actress."

"If you tell him that, he's sure to marry her."

"I hope the girl is good, Henry."

"Dorian says she's beautiful. We'll see her tonight."

"But do you approve[8], Henry?" asked Basil.

"You know I'm not a champion[9] of marriage. I hope that Dorian Gray will marry this girl, passionately[10] adore[11] her for six months, and then suddenly become fascinated[12] by someone else."

"You don't mean that[13], Henry."

Lord Henry laughed. "Of course, I mean it. But here's Dorian."

"My dear Henry, my dear Basil, you must both congratulate me!" said Dorian. "I've never been so happy. Come on. Let's go to the theater."

Marriage

- What do Dorian's friends think of his future marriage to Sibyl?
- Do you think this is a good sign?

The theater was crowded that night, and it was very hot.
"What a place to meet your love!" said Lord Henry.

"Don't worry! When Sibyl acts, you'll forget everything," said Dorian.

A quarter of an hour later, to huge applause[1], Sibyl Vane stepped on to the stage. Yes, she was lovely to look at.

"One of the loveliest girls I've ever seen," thought Lord Henry.

Basil Hallward stood up and began to applaud[2]. Dorian Gray sat gazing[3] at her. Sibyl Vane was beautiful, but she was strangely emotionless[4]. As Juliet she showed no sign of joy when she looked at Romeo, and she spoke unnaturally[5].

Dorian Gray grew pale as he watched her. He was puzzled[6] and worried. Neither of his friends said anything. The girl couldn't act. They were very disappointed. It wasn't nervousness. She was very confident[7]. It was simply bad acting. Even the audience lost interest in the play. They began to talk loudly and to whistle[8].

---

1 applause [əˈplɔz] (n.) 鼓掌；喝采
2 applaud [əˈplɔd] (v.) 鼓掌
3 gaze [ɡez] (v.) 凝視；注視
4 emotionless [ɪˈmoʃənlɪs] (a.) 沒情感的
5 unnaturally [ʌnˈnætʃərəlɪ] (adv.) 不自然地
6 puzzled [ˈpʌzld] (a.) 困惑的
7 confident [ˈkɑnfədənt] (a.) 有信心的
8 whistle [ˈhwɪsl] (v.) 吹口哨

Lord Henry got up from his chair and put on his coat. "She's very beautiful, Dorian," he said, "but she can't act. Let's go."

"I'm going to watch the play to the end," answered Dorian, in a hard bitter[1] voice.

"My dear Dorian, I'm sure Miss Vane's ill," said Basil. "We'll come another night."

"I wish she were ill," said Dorian. "But she looks well to me. She's changed. Last night she was a great actress. This evening she's a terrible actress."

"Let's go," said Lord Henry. "My dear boy, don't look so tragic[2]! Sibyl Vane is beautiful. What more do you want?

"Go away, Henry," said Dorian. "I want to be alone. Can't you see that my heart is breaking?" He hid his face in his hands.

"Let's go, Basil," said Lord Henry, and the two men left together.

As soon as the play was over, Dorian Gray ran backstage to the dressing room[3]. The girl stood there alone, with a look of triumph[4] on her face. When he entered, she smiled at him. "How badly I acted tonight, Dorian!" she cried happily.

"Horribly!" he answered, staring at her in amazement[5]. "It was awful[6]."

The girl smiled. "Dorian," she answered, "don't you understand?"

"Understand what?" he asked, angrily.

"Why I was so bad tonight."

He shrugged[7] his shoulders. "You're ill, I suppose. When you're ill you shouldn't act."

She didn't listen to him. She was happy. "Dorian," she cried, "Tonight, for the first time in my life, I saw the silliness[8] of the theater. I saw that the Romeo was ugly, and old, and painted, that the moonlight in the orchard[9] was false, and that the words I had to speak were unreal. They were not my words. You've made me understand what love really is. My love! Prince Charming! Prince of life! I'm tired of acting. When I came on tonight, I wanted to be wonderful. Then I found I couldn't act. I heard them talking, and I smiled. What do they know of love? Take me away, Dorian. I hate the stage. I can't act any more. I can't play at being in love. I am in love."

Dorian flung[10] himself down on the sofa. "You've killed my love," he said.

She came across to him and stroked[11] his hair. He leapt up and went to the door. "Without your art, you're nothing. I wanted to make you famous. I wanted the world to worship you. I wanted you to have my name. What are you now? A bad actress with a pretty face. I never want to see you again."

Sibyl went white. "You're not serious, Dorian?" she said. "You're acting."

---

1 bitter [ˋbɪtɚ] (a.) 極為不滿的
2 tragic [ˋtrædʒɪk] (a.) 悲慘的
3 dressing room 更衣室
4 triumph [ˋtraɪəmf] (n.) 勝利
5 amazement [əˋmezmənt] (n.) 吃驚
6 awful [ˋɔfʊl] (a.) 很糟糕的
7 shrug [ʃrʌg] (v.) 聳 (肩)
8 silliness [ˋsɪlɪnəs] (n.) 愚蠢
9 orchard [ˋɔrtʃəd] (n.) 果樹園
10 fling [flɪŋ] (v.) 扔；拋
   (三態：fling; flung; flung)
11 stroke [strok] (v.) 用手輕撫

"Acting! I'll leave that to you. You do it so well," he answered bitterly.

She ran across the room to him, and she put her hand on his arm and looked into his eyes.

"Don't touch me!" he cried.

"Dorian, don't leave me!" she whispered. "I can't bear it[1]. Can't you forgive[2] me for tonight? I've only acted badly once. Oh, please don't leave me."

She burst into tears[3], and Dorian Gray looked at her with disdain[4]. Her tears annoyed him. "I'm going," he said at last in his calm[5] voice. "I don't want to be unkind, but I can't see you again. You've disappointed me[6]."

She wept silently[7], and made no answer. He left the room.

Disdain

- What different side of Dorian's character do we see here?
- What do YOU think of Dorian's reaction[8]? Tell a friend.

In a few moments, Dorian was out of the theater. He wandered[9] through the dark streets, past black doors and evil-looking houses. As dawn broke[10], he hailed[11] a carriage[12] and drove home.

At home, he took off his hat and coat and walked through the library towards the door of his bedroom. As he was turning the handle of the door, he saw the portrait. He was shocked. He went over to the picture and examined it.

The expression[13] looked different. There were lines of cruelty[14] around the mouth. It was very strange.

---

1 I can't bear it. 我受不了。

2 forgive [fəˋgɪv] (v.) 原諒（三態：forgive; forgave; forgiven）

3 burst into tears 突然哭出來

4 disdain [dɪsˋden] (n.) 輕蔑；鄙視

5 calm [kɑm] (a.) 平靜的

6 disappoint [ˏdɪsəˋpɔɪnt] (v.) 使失望

7 silently [ˋsaɪləntlɪ] (adv.) 沉默地

8 reaction [rɪˋækʃən] (n.) 反應

9 wander [ˋwɑndɚ] (v.) 閒逛

10 break [brek] (v.)（天空）破曉（三態：break; broke; broken）

11 hail [hel] (v.) 招呼

12 carriage [ˋkærɪdʒ] (n.) 馬車

13 expression [ɪkˋsprɛʃən] (n.) 表情

14 cruelty [ˋkruəltɪ] (n.) 殘酷

He picked up a mirror from the table. There were no lines on his lips. What did it mean? He examined the picture again. There was no doubt that the expression was different. He sat down to think.

Suddenly he remembered his words in Basil Hallward's studio the day the picture was finished. "I wished I could stay young," he thought, "and the portrait could grow old. I wanted my beauty to stay the same, and the face on the canvas to change. I wanted to keep the loveliness of my youth. Has my wish been fulfilled[1]? It's impossible. And, yet, the picture has changed. There is definitely[2] a touch[3] of cruelty in the mouth. Cruelty! Have I been cruel? It was the girl's fault, not mine. She disappointed me."

Then he remembered her lying at his feet sobbing[4] like a little child. "I was cruel to her. That was unforgivable[5]. But I suffered too. Why should I worry about Sibyl Vane?"

Then he looked at the portrait with its cruel smile. "It's already changed. For every sin[6] that I commit[7], a stain[8] will spoil its beauty. But I won't sin again. I'll say sorry to Sibyl and marry her. My love for her will return.'

He got up from his chair and drew a large screen[9] in front of the portrait. Then he walked across to the window and opened it. The fresh morning air drove away all his dark thoughts.

---

1 fulfill [fʊlˋfɪl] (v.) 履行；實現
2 definitely [ˋdɛfənɪtlɪ] (adv.) 明確地
3 touch [tʌtʃ] (n.) 少許；一點
4 sob [sɑb] (v.) 啜泣；哭訴
5 unforgivable [ˌʌnfəˋgɪvəbl̩] (a.) 不可原諒的

6 sin [sɪn] (n.)（宗教或道德的）罪
(v.) 犯（罪）
7 commit [kəˋmɪt] (v.) 犯（罪）
8 stain [sten] (n.) 污點；瑕疵
9 screen [skrin] (n.) 屏風

Chapter 6

It was past noon when Dorian woke up. Last night's tragedy[1] felt like a dream. He got dressed, and then he went into the library and sat down to breakfast. He had a letter from Lord Henry, but he decided not to open it. It was a lovely day, and he felt happy. Then he looked at the screen in front of the portrait, and he jumped.

Dorian got up quickly and locked both doors. Then he drew the screen aside[2] and looked at the face.

It was true. The portrait was different.

"The good thing is, it's made me realize how cruel I was to Sibyl Vane," he thought. "It's not too late to put that right[3]. She can still be my wife. This portrait will guide[4] me through life. It will be my conscience[5]."

The clock struck three, then four, but Dorian Gray did not move.

Finally, he sat at the table and wrote a passionate[6] letter to Sibyl. He begged her to forgive him.

Conscience

- How is the portrait like Dorian's conscience?
- What does YOUR conscience tell you to do? Explain to a friend.

Suddenly there was a knock on the door, and he heard Lord Henry's voice outside. "My dear boy, I must see you. Let me in."

He jumped up, and quickly drew the screen across the picture. Then he unlocked the door.

"I'm so sorry, Dorian," said Lord Henry as he entered. "But you must not think too much about it."

"Do you mean about Sibyl Vane?" asked Dorian.

"Yes, of course," answered Lord Henry. "It's awful, but it wasn't your fault. Did you go backstage to see her, after the play?"

"Yes."

"Did you argue[7] with her?"

"I was very cruel to her, Henry. But it's all right now. I have learnt a lot about myself."

"Ah, Dorian, I'm so glad you see it that way! I thought you'd be very upset."

"I'm happy now," said Dorian, smiling. "I know what conscience is now and I want to be good. I hate the idea of my soul being evil."

"That's charming! I congratulate you, Dorian. But how are you going to begin?"

"By marrying Sibyl Vane."

---

1 tragedy [ˈtrædʒədɪ] (n.) 悲劇性事件
2 aside [əˈsaɪd] (adv.) 到旁邊
3 put that right 改善；挽回
4 guide [gaɪd] (v.) 指引
5 conscience [ˈkɑnʃəns] (n.) 良心
6 passionate [ˈpæʃənɪt] (a.) 熱烈的
7 argue [ˈɑrgjʊ] (v.) 爭吵

"Marrying Sibyl Vane!" cried Lord Henry, standing up and looking at him in amazement. "But, my dear Dorian, didn't you get my letter?"

"Your letter? Oh, yes, I remember. I haven't read it yet, Henry."

"You don't know then?"

"What do you mean?"

Guess

- What do you think Lord Henry's letter says?

Lord Henry walked across the room, and sitting down by Dorian Gray, took both his hands in his own. "Dorian," he said, "Don't be frightened. My letter was to tell you that Sibyl Vane is dead."

A cry of pain broke from Dorian's lips. "Dead! Sibyl dead! It's not true!"

"It is true, Dorian," said Lord Henry. "It's in all the morning newspapers. There will have to be an inquest[1], of course, and you must not be mixed up in[2] it. Do they know your name at the theater? If they don't, it's all right."

Dorian did not answer for a few moments. He was dazed[3] with horror.

Finally, he said, "Henry, did you say an inquest? Did Sibyl . . .? Oh, Henry, I can't bear it!"

"It wasn't an accident, Dorian. As she was leaving the theater with her mother, she went back upstairs for something. They waited for her, but she didn't come down again. They found her lying dead on the floor of her dressing room. They think that she drank some poison[4]."

"Henry, that's tragic!" cried Dorian.

"Yes, it is, but you mustn't get mixed up in it. Dorian, you mustn't let this upset you. You must come and dine with me, and afterwards we'll go to the opera. My sister's got a box[5]."

"So, I've murdered[6] Sibyl Vane," said Dorian, "but the birds still sing happily in my garden. And tonight I'll dine with you, and then go on to the opera. How extraordinary life is! Oh, Henry, how I loved her! She was everything to me. Then came that awful night—was it really only last night? She acted badly and I left her.

"Then something happened that made me afraid," Dorian continued. "I decided to go back to her. And now she's dead. My God! Henry, what shall I do? You don't know the danger I'm in. Now there's nothing to keep me straight[7]."

1 inquest [ˈɪnˌkwɛst] (n.) 審訊
2 be/get mixed up in sth 捲入不好的事件中
3 dazed [dezd] (a.) 暈眩的；茫然的
4 poison [ˈpɔɪzn̩] (n.) 毒藥
5 box [bɑks] (n.) （戲院）包廂
6 murder [ˈmɝdɚ] (v.) 謀殺；兇殺
7 straight [stret] (a.) 正直的

"My dear Dorian," answered Lord Henry, "You are more fortunate than I am. Not one of the women I've loved has killed themselves for me."

"I was very cruel to Sibyl. You forget that."

Then there was silence. The evening darkened the room, and the shadows[1] crept[2] in from the garden.

After some time, Dorian Gray looked up. "We won't talk of my love again. It was a wonderful experience. That's all."

"Now let's go to the club and eat. It's late," said Lord Henry.

"I'll join you at the opera, Henry. I feel too tired to eat anything. What is the number of your sister's box?"

"Twenty-seven. You'll see her name on the door."

"Thank you for all that you've said to me," said Dorian. "You're my best friend."

"We're only at the beginning of our friendship, Dorian," answered Lord Henry. "Now, goodbye. I'll see you later."

Dark

- Find the references[3] to the dark and shadows. What do you think they represent[4]?

---

1 shadow [ˈʃædo] (n.) 陰影
2 creep [krip] (v.) 爬行；蔓延
  （三態：creep; crept; crept）
3 reference [ˈrɛfərəns] (n.) 關聯
4 represent [ˌrɛprɪˈzɛnt] (v.) 代表

5 miserable [ˈmɪzərəb!] (a.)
  痛苦的；悽慘的
6 It's all in the past. 一切已成往事。
7 as if 彷彿

Chapter 7

As Dorian was having breakfast the next morning, Basil Hallward was shown into the room.

"I'm so glad I've found you, Dorian," he said. "I called last night, and they told me you were at the opera. Of course, I knew that was impossible. I read about Sibyl's death in a newspaper. I came here at once. I know you must be miserable[5]. But where were you? Did you go and see the girl's mother? Poor woman! She must be very upset! What did she say about it all?"

"My dear Basil, how do I know?" said Dorian. "I was at the opera. I met Lady Gwendolen, Henry's sister, for the first time. We were in her box. She's charming."

"You went to the opera?" said Basil, shocked. "You went to the opera while Sibyl Vane was lying dead? How can you talk to me of other women being charming when the girl you loved is dead?"

"Stop, Basil! I won't listen!" said Dorian. "It's all in the past[6] now."

"You call yesterday the past? Dorian, this is horrible! Something has changed you. You talk as if[7] you have no heart. It's all Henry's influence. I never see you nowadays. You must come and sit for me again."

"I can never sit for you again, Basil," Dorian exclaimed.

Basil stared at him. "Why not?" he asked. "Don't you like my portrait of you? Where is it? Why have you pulled the screen in front of it? Let me look at it. Take the screen away, Dorian. Let me see the portrait."

"No," Dorian cried out in terror, and he ran between Basil and the screen. "You mustn't look at it."

"Why can't I look at the portrait?" asked Basil, laughing.

"If you look at it, Basil, I'll never speak to you again."

Basil looked at Dorian in amazement. "But I'm going to exhibit it in Paris in the autumn."

Dorian was scared[1]. "You said you didn't want to exhibit it," he cried. "Why have you changed your mind[2]? Why didn't you want to exhibit my picture before?"

Basil looked worried. "Have you noticed something strange about the picture?"

"Basil!" cried Dorian, with a look of fear[3] in his eyes.

"I see you have. Don't speak. Dorian, from the moment I met you, your personality[4] had an extraordinary influence over me. Then one fatal[5] day, I decided to paint a portrait of you. I put everything into that painting, and I felt, Dorian, that there was too much of myself in the painting. So I decided never to exhibit it. A few days later, the portrait left my studio. Then I felt it was all in my imagination. It's just a good painting. That's all. You're very good-looking and I'm a good artist. And so when I got this offer[6] from Paris, I decided to show your portrait in my exhibition. But you're right. I won't exhibit it."

---

1 scared [skɛrd] (a.) 吃驚的；嚇壞的
2 change one's mind 改變心意
3 fear [fɪr] (n.) 害怕；擔心
4 personality [ˌpɝsṇˋælətɪ] (n.) 人格
5 fatal [ˋfetḷ] (a.) 命中注定的
6 offer [ˋɔfɚ] (n.) 提供；提議

Dorian smiled. The danger was over. He was safe for the moment.

"Can I look at the portrait now?" asked Basil.

Dorian shook his head.

"Well, perhaps you're right. I must go now."

As he left the room, Dorian smiled to himself. "Poor Basil! He doesn't know the true reason!" He sighed and rang the bell. "I must hide the portrait. No one must see it," he thought.

Mrs Leaf, the housekeeper[1] entered, and Dorian asked her for the key of the schoolroom[2].

"The old schoolroom, Mr Dorian?" she exclaimed. "But it's full of dust[3]. No one has been in there for five years."

"That doesn't matter," Dorian answered. "I want to see the place—that's all. Give me the key."

"Here's the key, Sir," said the old lady.

"Thank you, Mrs Leaf. That's all."

As the door closed, Dorian put the key in his pocket and looked round the room. His eye fell on a large, purple cloth[4]. He picked it up and walked behind the screen.

"I hate this portrait," he thought, and with a look of pain, he threw[5] the cloth over the picture.

Then he took the picture upstairs to the old schoolroom.

"This room will keep the secret of my life. No one will see the portrait here. I won't see it. I don't want to watch the corruption[6] of my soul," he thought.

Dorian left the room and locked the door again. He felt safe now.

Soul

- Go back to page 27. What does say Dorian about his soul?

- What is slowly happening to Dorian's soul? Underline the word "soul" whenever you notice it in the story.

---

1 housekeeper [ˈhaʊsˌkipɚ] (n.) 女管家

2 schoolroom [ˈskulˌrum] (n.) 書房

3 dust [dʌst] (n.) 灰塵

4 cloth [klɔθ] (n.) 布

5 throw [θro] (v.) 丟；投；扔
（三態：throw; threw; thrown）

6 corruption [kəˈrʌpʃən] (n.) 墮落

Chapter 8

The years passed and Dorian remained beautiful and young. From time to time[1], strange stories about his way of life crept through London. But he looked so innocent[2] that nobody could believe anything bad of him.

He often crept upstairs to the locked room, and he stood with a mirror in front of the portrait. He looked at the evil and ageing[3] face on the canvas, and then at his beautiful young face in the mirror. The contrast[4] made him happy. He loved his good looks, and found the corruption of his soul interesting.

Summer followed summer, and the flowers in his garden bloomed[5] and died many times, but Dorian was unchanged.

Then something happened. It was on the ninth of November, the night before Dorian Gray's thirty-eighth birthday. It was about eleven o'clock. Dorian was walking home when a man passed him in the fog[6]. Dorian recognized[7] the man. It was Basil Hallward. A strange feeling of fear came over him. He didn't say hello. He walked on, but Basil recognized him.

"Dorian! This is lucky! I've just come from your house. I'm going to Paris on the midnight train, and I wanted to see you before I left. Didn't you recognize me?"

"Not in this fog," Dorian replied. "I can't even recognize my house. I'm sorry you're going away. Will you be back soon?"

"No, I'm going away for six months. I want to take a studio in Paris. Well, here we are at your door. Let me come in for a moment. I need to talk to you."

"Of course, but won't you miss your train?" asked Dorian as he walked up the steps and opened the door.

"I've got plenty of time," he answered. "The train doesn't leave till twelve fifteen, and it's only eleven."

Dorian looked at him and smiled. "Come in."

Basil followed Dorian into the library.

"Now," Basil began. "I want to speak to you seriously."

"What do you want to talk to me about?" said Dorian. "I hope it isn't about me."

"It is about you," answered Basil. "People are saying the most terrible things about you."

"I don't want to know."

"But Dorian, you don't want people to talk badly about you. Of course, I don't believe the stories about you. Sin writes itself across a man's face. You can't hide it. But you have a young and innocent face. I can't believe anything against you. They say that you corrupt[8] all your friends."

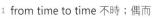

1 from time to time 不時；偶而
2 innocent [ˈɪnəsn̩t] (a.) 純真的
3 ageing [ˈedʒɪŋ] (a.) 變老的
4 contrast [ˈkɑn,træst] (n.) 對比
5 bloom [blum] (v.) 開花
6 fog [fɑg] (n.) 霧
7 recognize [ˈrɛkəg,naɪz] (v.) 認出
8 corrupt [kəˈrʌpt] (v.) 使墮落

"Stop, Basil," said Dorian Gray.

"I must speak and you must listen. I wonder[1], do I really know you? Before I can answer that, I need to see your soul."

"To see my soul!" said Dorian Gray, turning white with fear.

"Yes," answered Basil. "I need to see your soul. But only God can do that."

A bitter laugh broke from Dorian's lips. "Come with me, and I'll show you my soul. It's your handiwork[2]."

Basil stepped back.

Dorian smiled. He took a candle from the table. "Come upstairs, Basil," he said quietly. "I keep a diary[3] of my life. I'll show it to you."

"Okay, Dorian. I'll come and see it. But I can't read anything tonight. All I want is a plain[4] answer to my question."

"You'll find that upstairs, and you won't have to read anything."

---

1 wonder [ˈwʌndə] (v.) 想知道；納悶
2 handiwork [ˈhændɪˌwɝk] (n.) 手工藝品
3 keep a diary 寫日記
4 plain [plen] (a.) 清楚明白的

5 reach [ritʃ] (v.) 到達；來到
6 damp [dæmp] (n.) 潮濕 (a.) 潮濕的
7 exclamation [ˌɛksklə`meʃən] (n.) 叫喊
8 hideous [ˈhɪdɪəs] (a.) 醜陋的；可怕的

Chapter 9

Dorian Gray walked out of the room and began to climb the stairs. Basil Hallward followed him. The candle made shadows on the wall. When they reached[5] the top, Dorian unlocked a door.

"Do you still want to see, Basil?" he asked.

"Yes." said Basil.

"Good," he answered, smiling. Then he added, "You're the one man in the world who should know everything about me. You've had more influence on my life than you think."

Then he opened the door and went in.

"Shut the door behind you," he whispered.

Basil looked around him with a puzzled expression. The whole room was covered with dust and there was a smell of damp[6].

"So you think that it is only God who sees the soul, Basil? Pull that cloth off, and you'll see my soul," said Dorian in a cold, cruel voice.

"You're mad, Dorian." said Basil.

"If you won't pull off the cloth, then I will do it myself," said Dorian, and he threw the cloth on the ground.

An exclamation[7] of horror broke from Basil's lips when he saw the hideous[8] face on the canvas.

Good heavens! It was Dorian Gray's face! You could still see some gold in the thinning hair[1] and the eyes were still a lovely blue. Yes, it was Dorian. But who painted it? It looked like his work.

Basil seized the candle, and held it to the painting. His name was in the left-hand corner, in long red letters. This was his painting. He felt cold with fear.

He turned and looked at Dorian Gray. "What does this mean?" he cried.

"Years ago, when I was a boy," said Dorian Gray, "you flattered[2] me, and you taught me to be vain. One day, you introduced me to a friend of yours, who explained to me the importance of youth. Then you finished a portrait of me that showed me the wonder[3] of beauty. In a mad moment, I made a wish . . ."

"I remember your wish! No! It's impossible. The room is damp. Damp has spoilt the canvas. Maybe the paints had some mineral[4] poison in them. Paintings can't change. It's impossible. You told me you destroyed the portrait."

"I was wrong," said Dorian. "It has destroyed me."

"I don't believe it's my painting. There was nothing evil in my portrait. This is the face of evil."

"It's the face of my soul."

"It has the eyes of a devil."

"Each of us has heaven and hell in him, Basil," cried Dorian.

---

1 thinning hair 稀疏的頭髮

2 flatter [ˋflætɚ] (v.) 奉承；使高興

3 wonder [ˋwʌndɚ] (n.) 驚奇；驚異

4 mineral [ˋmɪnərəl] (a.) 礦物的

Basil turned again to the portrait and stared at it.

"My God! If it's true," Basil exclaimed, "you must be worse than they say you are!"

He held the light up again and examined the canvas. The surface[1] was the same. The evil was coming from within[2]. Sin was slowly eating the portrait away[3].

His hand shook, and the candle fell to the floor. He placed his foot on it and put it out[4]. He could hear Dorian sobbing at the window.

Heaven and hell

- Dorian says: "Each of us has heaven and hell in him." Do you agree? Discuss with a partner.

"Pray[5], Dorian." Basil said.

Dorian Gray turned slowly around. "It's too late, Basil." he cried.

"It's never too late, Dorian. Let's pray."

Dorian Gray looked at the picture, and suddenly he felt hatred[6] for Basil Hallward. The image on the canvas whispered in his ear. He looked wildly around the room. He saw a knife that he once brought up to the old schoolroom. He moved slowly towards it, and picked it up.

1 surface [ˋsɝfɪs] (n.) 表面
2 within [wɪˋðɪn] (n.) 內部
3 eat away 侵蝕
4 put out 撲滅
5 pray [pre] (v.) 祈禱
6 hatred [ˋhetrɪd] (n.) 憎恨；敵意
7 rush at 衝向
8 stab [stæb] (v.) 刺；刺傷
9 drip [drɪp] (n.) 水滴

The Picture of Dorian Gray

Then Dorian rushed at[7] Basil, and he stabbed[8] him. There was a loud cry. Dorian stabbed Basil again and again.

He waited for a moment. Then he threw the knife on the table. The house was quiet. He could hear nothing, but the drip[9] of blood on the floor.

"How quickly I killed him!" he thought.

Dorian felt strangely calm. He didn't look at the murdered man. He walked out of the room, and he locked the door behind him. Then he crept quietly downstairs.

When he reached the library, he pulled out his watch. It was twenty to two.

He sat down and began to think. What evidence[1] was there against him? "Basil left the house at eleven," he thought. "No one saw him come in again. My valet[2] was in bed . . . Paris! Yes. Basil went to Paris on the midnight train."

Dorian put on his fur[3] coat and hat, and he went outside. Then he rang the bell. In about five minutes his valet, Francis, appeared.

"I'm sorry to wake you up, Francis," he said, "but I forgot my key. What time is it?"

"Ten past two, Sir," answered the valet.

"Ten past two? It's late! You must wake me at nine tomorrow. I've got some work to do."

"All right, Sir."

"Did anyone call this evening?"

"Mr Hallward, Sir. He stayed here till eleven, and then he went to catch his train[4]."

"Oh! I'm sorry I didn't see him. Did he leave a message[5]?"

"No, Sir. He'll write to you from Paris."

"Thank you, Francis. Good night."

Dorian Gray threw his hat and coat on the table and walked into the library.

For a quarter of an hour he walked up and down the room, thinking. Then he took down the Blue Book[6] from one of the shelves[7] and began to turn the pages.

"Alan Campbell, 152, Hertford Street, Mayfair."

Yes, that was the man he wanted.

Chapter 10

At nine o'clock the next morning, his valet came in with a cup of chocolate and opened the curtains. The pale November sun shone into the room. Slowly Dorian began to remember the horrible events[8] of last night. He still felt hatred for Basil Hallward.

"He made me kill him." he thought.

Now the dead man was still there. That was horrible! He mustn't think about it.

He got up quickly and got dressed. He spent a long time at breakfast. Then he sat at his writing desk and he wrote two letters. One he put in his pocket, the other he handed to the valet.

"Francis, take this to Mr Campbell at 152, Hertford Street."

"What if Alan Campbell isn't in England? What shall I do then?" he thought.

They were great friends in the past. But when they met now, it was only Dorian Gray who smiled. Alan Campbell never did.

Campbell was a very clever young man. He loved science, and he had a laboratory[9] of his own. They both loved music, and they went to the opera and concerts[10] together.

---

1 evidence [ˈɛvədəns] (n.) 證據
2 valet [ˈvælɪt] (n.) 貼身男僕
3 fur [fɝ] (n.) 毛；皮
4 catch a train 趕火車
5 leave a message 留言
6 Blue Book 姓名地址簿
7 shelf [ʃɛlf] (n.) (書櫥等的) 架子 (複數形：shelves)
8 event [ɪˈvɛnt] (n.) 事件
9 laboratory [ˈlæbrəˌtorɪ] (n.) 實驗室
10 concert [ˈkɑnsət] (n.) 音樂會

Their friendship lasted for eighteen months. Then suddenly their friendship ended and people talked about it. If Dorian Gray came to a party, Alan Campbell left early. He changed, too—he looked sad, and he didn't play the piano any more. This was the man Dorian Gray was waiting for. Every second, Dorian looked at the clock. He was very nervous. His hands were cold.

At last, Alan Campbell arrived. He looked very stern[1] and pale.

"Alan!" said Dorian. "This is kind of you. Thank you for coming."

"I didn't want to enter your house again, Gray. But you said it was a matter of life and death." His voice was hard and cold.

"Yes, it is, Alan. Sit down."

Campbell took a chair by the table, and Dorian sat opposite[2] him. "Alan, in a locked room at the top of this house, there is a dead man. He has been dead for ten hours now . . ."

"Stop, Gray. I don't want to know anything more. Keep your horrible secrets to yourself."

"Alan, you can save me. You know about chemistry[3]. You do strange experiments[4]. You must destroy the body upstairs. Nobody saw this person come into the house. People think he's in Paris. Alan, you must change him into ashes[5]."

"You're mad, Dorian. I won't help you."

---

1 stern [stɝn] (a.) 嚴厲的
2 opposite [`ɑpəzɪt] (prep.) 在對面
3 chemistry [`kɛmɪstrɪ] (n.) 化學
4 experiment [ɪk`spɛrəmənt] (n.) 實驗
5 ash [æʃ] (n.) 灰燼；骨灰

49

"Alan, it was murder. I killed him." said Dorian.

"Murder! Good God, Dorian, are you a murderer now?"

"I just want you to destroy the body. This body is the only evidence against me. Please, help me. We were friends once. They'll arrest me, Alan! Don't you understand?"

"I refuse to help you."

"You refuse?"

"Yes."

Then a look of pity[6] came into Dorian Gray's eyes. He took a piece of paper, and wrote something on it. He read it twice. Then he handed it to Campbell.

As he read it, his face went pale.

"I'm sorry, Alan," said Dorian. "But I have no alternative[7]. I have already written a letter. Here it is. You see the address. If you don't help me, I'll send it. You can't refuse now."

Alan hesitated[8] a moment. "Is there a fire in the room upstairs?"

"Yes, there is," Dorian replied.

"I'll have to go home and get some things from the laboratory."

"No, Alan, you can't leave the house. My servant will take a carriage to your house and bring the things back to you."

The two men waited in silence for the servant to return. The minutes ticked[9] slowly by on the clock.

---

6 pity [ˋpɪtɪ] (n.) 憐憫;同情
7 alternative [ɔlˋtɝnətɪv] (n.) 選擇
8 hesitate [ˋhɛzəˌtet] (v.) 躊躇;猶豫
9 tick [tɪk] (v.) 發出滴答聲

At last, there was a knock on the door, and the servant entered. He had a large chest[1] of chemicals, some metal wire[2] and two iron clamps[3].

"Shall I leave the things here, Sir?" he asked Campbell.

"Yes." said Campbell. Then the servant left the room.

"Now, Alan, we must be quick," said Dorian. "Follow me upstairs."

Dorian unlocked the door to the room. He looked scared. "I don't think I can go in, Alan," he said.

"I don't need you." said Campbell coldly.

Dorian half opened the door, and he saw the horrible face of his portrait. On the floor in front of it, lay the purple cloth.

"I forgot to hide the horrible portrait," he thought. "I must cover it now."

Then he saw a red drop of blood on one of the hands. It was horrible. He walked quickly into the room. Then, he picked up the cloth, and he threw it over the painting.

Campbell brought in the heavy chest, and the clamps.

"Leave me now," said Campbell.

Dorian turned and hurried out of the room. Campbell looked at the dead face of Basil Hallward. As Dorian walked downstairs, he heard Campbell lock the door.

It was after seven when Campbell came back into the library. He was pale, but calm.

"I've done it," he said. "And now, goodbye. I never want to see you again."

"You've saved my life, Alan. I can't forget that." said Dorian.

After Campbell left, Dorian went upstairs. There was a horrible smell of nitric acid[4] in the room, but the body was gone.

Life

- Do you think Dorian's life is worth saving? Discuss in groups.

---

1 chest [tʃɛst] (n.) 箱子
2 metal wire 金屬導線
3 iron clamp 鐵挾
4 nitric acid [ˈnaɪtrɪk ˈæsɪd] 硝酸

Chapter 11

At midnight, Dorian Gray crept quietly out of his house. A cold rain fell, and there was a thick fog. Dorian Gray took a carriage to a tavern[1] near the harbor[2].

"An innocent man has died," he thought. "For that there is no forgiveness[3]. Forgiveness is impossible, but forgetfulness[4] is still possible."

In one corner of the tavern, a sailor sat with his head in his arms on a table, and by the bar, stood two haggard[5] women.

As he entered, one of the two women with painted lips laughed out loud.

"There goes the devil!" she said.

"Don't call me that." Dorian said and he decided to leave.

"Prince Charming is what you like to be called, isn't it?" she shouted after him.

The sailor at the table jumped to his feet as she spoke, and looked round. He heard the tavern door shut. He ran outside.

Dorian Gray hurried along the quay[6] through the rain. Suddenly, he felt a hand on his shoulder. He was pushed against the wall. Then a hand was round his neck. He struggled[7] for his life. Then he heard the click[8] of a gun. The gun was pointed straight at his head.

---

1 tavern ['tævɚn] (n.) 小酒館
2 harbor ['hɑrbɚ] (n.) 港口；海港
3 forgiveness [fɚ'gɪvnɪs] (n.) 寬恕
4 forgetfulness [fɚ'gɛtfəlnɪs] (n.) 遺忘

5 haggard ['hægɚd] (a.) 憔悴的
6 quay [ki] (n.) 碼頭
7 struggle ['strʌgl̩] (v.) 掙扎
8 click [klɪk] (n.) 喀嚓聲

"What do you want?" Dorian cried.

"Keep quiet," said the man. "If you move, I'll shoot[1] you."

"You're mad. What have I done to you?"

Sailor

- Who do you think this man is?

"You destroyed the life of Sibyl Vane," was the answer, "and Sibyl Vane was my sister. She killed herself. Her death is your fault. Now I will kill you. For years, I've searched[2] for you, but I couldn't find you. The only thing I knew about you was your pet name[3]. I heard it tonight, 'Prince Charming'."

Dorian Gray felt sick with fear. "I've never heard of her," he said. "You're mad."

"Down on your knees!" shouted the man. "My ship sails for India tonight, and I must kill you first."

Dorian was scared. He didn't know what to do. Suddenly, he had an idea.

"Stop," he cried. "When did your sister die? Quick, tell me!"

"Eighteen years ago," said the man. "Why do you ask me?"

---

1 shoot [ʃut] (v.) 開槍（三態：shoot; shot; shot）
2 search [sɜtʃ] (v.) 尋找
3 pet name 暱稱

"Eighteen years ago," laughed Dorian Gray. "But look at my face!"

James Vane hesitated for a moment. Then he stared[1] at Dorian Gray's face. This was the face of a twenty-year-old boy.

"He was only a little older than my sister was when I sailed for Australia," he thought. "This can't be the man who destroyed her life."

Then he stepped back.

"My God!" he cried, "I nearly murdered you!"

Dorian Gray breathed a sigh of relief[2]. "This is a warning to you. Don't take vengeance[3] into your own hands."

"Forgive me, Sir," said James Vane. "I was wrong."

"Go home and put that gun away." said Dorian. Then he turned and walked slowly down the street.

James Vane stood and looked at him in horror. He was shaking from head to foot[4].

After a little while[5], a black shadow moved out into the light and came close to him. He felt a hand on his arm, and he looked round. It was one of the women from the bar.

"Why didn't you kill him? You fool! He has lots of money, and he's bad."

"He isn't the man I'm looking for," James answered. "I'm not interested in money. I want a man's life. The man I want must be nearly forty now. This one is too young."

The woman gave a bitter laugh. "Young!" she sneered[6]. "It's nearly eighteen years since I met Prince Charming."

"You lie!" cried James Vane.

"I'm telling the truth," she cried. "They say he has sold himself to the devil[7] for a pretty face. He hasn't changed at all in eighteen years," she added.

"Is this the truth?"

"Yes, it's the truth. But don't tell him," she cried. "I'm afraid of him."

James Vane ran to the corner of the street but Dorian Gray wasn't there.

Vengeance

- What did James Vane promise to do to Prince Charming? Go back to pages 41 and 42 to check.

---

1 stare [stɛr] (v.) 盯；凝視
2 relief [rɪˋlif] (n.) 緩和；解除
3 vengeance [ˋvɛndʒəns] (n.) 報復；復仇
4 from head to foot 從頭到腳
5 after a little while 一會兒後
6 sneer [snɪr] (v.) 冷笑；譏諷
7 devil [ˋdɛv!] (n.) 魔鬼；惡魔

Chapter 12

A week later Dorian Gray was at his country house with a party of friends. They were having dinner. Dorian laughed and smiled, but now and then he felt afraid. Suddenly he looked around and he saw James Vane's face close to the window. Dorian Gray looked away and when he looked back the face was gone.

"Maybe I imagined it," Dorian thought. "The servants haven't reported a stranger near the house. I just imagined it. Sibyl Vane's brother hasn't come back to kill me. He's sailed away on his ship. I'm safe."

The next day, Dorian drove across the park to join a shooting party[1].

The frost[2] lay like salt on the grass, and the sky was blue. At the corner of the wood, he saw his friend Sir Geoffrey, with his gun. He walked over to join him. Suddenly a hare[3] ran out from behind a bush[4].

Sir Geoffrey put his gun to his shoulder, but there was something about the animal that Dorian Gray liked.

"Don't shoot it, Geoffrey," he cried.

Sir Geoffrey laughed. Then, as the hare jumped into the bushes, he fired. They heard two cries, the cry of a hare in pain, and the cry of a man in agony[5].

---

1 shooting party 狩獵隊
2 frost [frɑst] (n.) 霜
3 hare [hɛr] (n.) 野兔
4 bush [buʃ] (n.) 灌木叢 (v.) 叢生
5 agony [ˈægənɪ] (n.) 極度痛苦；苦惱

"Good heavens! I've hit a man!" exclaimed Sir Geoffrey. "Stop shooting!" he called out at the top of his voice. "A man is hurt."

The gamekeeper[1] came running up. "Where, Sir? Where is he?" he shouted.

"Here," answered Sir Geoffrey angrily, running towards the bushes.

Dorian watched them. In a few moments they came out, pulling a body after them. He turned away in horror.

"Is the man dead?" asked Sir Geoffrey.

"Yes." replied the gamekeeper.

After a few moments, Dorian felt a hand on his shoulder. He turned round.

"Dorian," said Lord Henry. "Come on. Let's go home."

They walked side by side without speaking.

Then Dorian looked at Lord Henry and said, with a sigh, "It's a bad omen[2], Henry. Something horrible is going to happen to me."

The elder man laughed. "What on earth[3] could happen to you, Dorian?"

"Don't laugh like that. I want to escape[4]. I'll tell Harvey to get the yacht[5] ready. I'll be safe on the yacht."

"Safe from what, Dorian? Are you in trouble? Tell me. You know I'll help you."

"I can't tell you, Henry," answered Dorian sadly. "Now I must go and lie down. I feel tired."

Trouble

- When YOU are in trouble who do you like to talk to?
- Do you think talking to other people helps you?
  Tell a friend.

When Dorian was resting[6] in his room, the gamekeeper came to see him.

"Have you come about the accident this morning, Thornton?" Dorian asked him.

"Yes, Sir," answered the gamekeeper.

"Was the poor man married? Does he have any children?" asked Dorian. "I'd like to send them some money."

"We don't know who he is, Sir. He looks like a sailor."

"A sailor?" Dorian cried. "Did you say a sailor?"

"Yes, Sir. He's got tattoos[7] on both arms."

Dorian stood up. "Where's the body?" he asked. "Quick! I must see it at once."

"It's in an empty stable[8] on the Home Farm, Sir."

1 gamekeeper [ˈgem,kipɚ] (n.) 獵場看守人
2 omen [ˈomən] (n.) 預兆
3 on earth 究竟
4 escape [əˈskep] (v.) 逃跑
5 yacht [jɑt] (n.) 遊艇
6 rest [rɛst] (v.) 休息
7 tattoo [tæˈtu] (n.) 刺青
8 stable [ˈstebḷ] (n.) 馬廄

"The Home Farm! Go there immediately and I'll follow."

In less than quarter of an hour, Dorian Gray was galloping[1] down the long road on his horse. The stones flew as he rode. At last he reached the Home Farm.

In one of the stables, there was a light. He hurried to the door and was about to open it. Then he paused for a moment. This discovery would either make or ruin[2] his life.

Then he opened the door and entered. The dead man lay in the far corner. There was a spotted[3] handkerchief over the face. Dorian Gray called out to one of the farm servants.

"Take that handkerchief off his face. I want to see it," he said.

The farm servant lifted the handkerchief and Dorian Gray gave a cry of joy.

The man was James Vane.

Dorian stood there for some minutes looking at the dead body.

As he rode home, his eyes were full of tears, because he knew he was safe.

1 gallop [ˈgæləp] (v.) 騎馬奔馳
2 ruin [ˈrʊɪn] (v.) 毀滅
3 spotted [ˈspɑtɪd] (a.) 斑點的；斑紋的
4 divorce [dəˈvors] (n.) 離婚
5 suicide [ˈsuəˌsaɪd] (n.) 自殺
6 have no idea 不知道

Chapter 13

A few weeks later, Dorian visited Lord Henry.

"Don't tell me you're going to be good," cried Lord Henry. "You're perfect already. You don't need to change."

Dorian Gray shook his head. "I've done too many horrible things in my life. I'm not going to do any more. But let's not talk about me. What's going on in town? I haven't been to the club for days."

"People are still discussing Basil's disappearance."

"I thought they were tired of that now," said Dorian.

"My dear boy, they've only talked about it for six weeks. They have been very lucky recently. They've had my divorce[4] and Alan Campbell's suicide[5]."

"What do you think has happened to Basil?" asked Dorian calmly.

"I've no idea[6]."

"What if I told you that I murdered Basil?"

"You couldn't murder anyone, Dorian. But let's not talk about Basil. He probably fell into the Seine from a bus. By the way, where's that wonderful portrait he did of you? Oh! I remember now. You told me years ago that you sent it to Selby Manor and that it got lost or stolen on the way. What a pity! I wanted to buy it. I wish I had now."

"I never really liked it." said Dorian.

"How have you kept your youth, Dorian? You must have some secret. I'm only ten years older than you are, and I'm wrinkled and old. Please, tell me your secret. To get back my youth, I'd do anything in the world, except take exercise[1], get up early, or be respectable[2]."

Lord Henry

- What is Lord Henry NOT prepared to do to get back his youth?

When Dorian arrived home that night, he sent his servant to bed, and sat down on the sofa in the library. Then he began to think about his life.

"I've been an evil influence on my friends, and I've ruined the lives of many good young people," he thought. "Ah! Why did I pray for the portrait to grow old, and for me to stay young? I wanted beauty and eternal[3] youth, but they ruined me. It's better not to think of the past. Nothing can change that. I must think of the future. James Vane is dead. Alan Campbell is dead, too. He shot himself one night in his laboratory."

"I'm safe now," he continued. "Basil painted the portrait that ruined my life. I can't forgive him for that. Everything is the portrait's fault."

---

1 take exercise 從事運動
2 respectable [rɪ'spɛktəbl̩] (a.) 值得尊敬的
3 eternal [ɪ'tɝnl̩] (a.) 永恆的

He began to wonder about the portrait.

"If I'm good, maybe the portrait will become beautiful again," he thought. "I'll go and look."

He took the lamp from the table and went upstairs. As he unlocked the door, he smiled.

"Yes, I'll be good," he thought. "I won't be frightened of this portrait any more."

He went upstairs to the room and locked the door. Then he pulled the purple cloth off the portrait. He gave a cry of pain.

The portrait was more horrible. His face looked more evil. There was new blood on the hand and on the feet.

Good or evil

- Can Dorian be good? Or is it too late?

Dorian trembled[1] with fear.

"Should I confess[2] to Basil's murder?" he thought. "No. That's a stupid idea. There is only one piece of evidence against me—the portrait. I must destroy it. Why have I kept it so long? It's been my conscience, of course. But now I'll destroy it."

---

1 tremble [ˈtrɛmbl̩] (v.) 顫抖
2 confess [kənˈfɛs] (v.) 坦白；承認

Portrait

- On page 52, Dorian realizes his portrait is his conscience. He now wants to destroy it. Do YOU think it is possible to destroy one's conscience? Discuss in groups.

Dorian looked round the room and saw the knife that stabbed Basil Hallward. It was bright and shining.

"This knife killed the artist, and now it will kill the artist's work," he thought. "It will kill the past, and when that is dead, I'll be free."

He grabbed[1] the knife, and then he stabbed the portrait with it. There was a cry and a crash[2]. The cry was so horrible that the servants woke up, and they crept out of their rooms. They didn't know what to do. Old Mrs Leaf, the housekeeper, began to cry.

After about a quarter of an hour, Francis got two other servants and they crept upstairs. They knocked on the door of the room, but there was no reply[3]. They called out. There was no answer. They couldn't open the door. Finally, they climbed onto the roof and jumped down onto the balcony[4] outside the schoolroom. The windows opened easily—their locks were old.

---

1 grab [græb] (v.) 抓取
2 crash [kræʃ] (n.) 撞擊聲
3 reply [rɪ`plaɪ] (n.) 回應
4 balcony [`bælkənɪ] (n.) 陽臺；露臺

 When they entered, they saw a beautiful portrait of Dorian Gray as a young man. In front of it, there was a man lying dead on the floor.

 The man on the floor was wrinkled and old and he had an evil face.

 It was not till they examined the rings that they recognized who it was.

AFTER READING

Ⓐ Personal Response

1 What is important to the society in the book? Tick (✓).

- ⓐ youth and beauty
- ⓑ wit and intelligence
- ⓒ kindness and generosity

2 Agree (✓) or disagree (×) with the statements.

_____ ⓐ Lord Henry Wotton is a bad influence on Dorian Gray.

_____ ⓑ Basil Hallward is very unkind to Dorian Gray.

_____ ⓒ Dorian Gray is very cruel to Sibyl.

_____ ⓓ It was Sibyl's fault that Dorian left her.

_____ ⓔ Dorian Gray is a good friend to have.

_____ ⓕ Evil shows on people's faces.

3 Did you like the story? Why?/Why not?

4 Is there anything in the story that you would like to change? Give details.

5 Did you like the ending? Suggest another way in which the story could end.

❸ Comprehension

6 Tick (✓) true (T) or false (F).

T F　(a) The artist doesn't want to exhibit the portrait because it is a painting of himself.

T F　(b) Dorian falls in love with an actress, Sibyl Vane.

T F　(c) James Vane says he will kill Dorian if he hurts Sibyl.

T F　(d) Basil Hallward kills Sibyl.

T F　(e) Dorian decides to apologize to Sibyl but it's too late.

T F　(f) James Vane finds Dorian and shoots him.

7 Put the events from the story into the correct order.

(a) The portrait changes. Dorian's smile is cruel now.

(b) Dorian breaks Sibyl's heart.

(c) Basil Hallward paints a beautiful portrait of Dorian Gray.

(d) Dorian is angry with Basil Hallward. He murders him.

(e) Sibyl kills herself.

(f) Dorian Gray falls in love with the actress, Sibyl Vane.

(g) Dorian tries to destroy the portrait but he dies.

(h) There is now blood in the portrait.

8 Match the two halves of Lord Henry Wotton's sayings.

1️⃣ take exercise, get up early, or be respectable.
2️⃣ helping the sick and the poor.
3️⃣ to make it last forever.
4️⃣ the one thing worth having.
5️⃣ don't commit crimes.
6️⃣ has killed themselves for me.

____ a️⃣ Don't waste your golden days

____ b️⃣ Women spoil every romance by trying

____ c️⃣ People like you, Dorian

____ d️⃣ Youth is

____ e️⃣ Not one of the women I've loved

____ f️⃣ To get back my youth, I'd do anything in the world, except

9 Work with a partner. Try to remember how the things in these pictures are important to the story.

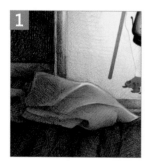  

C Characters

10 Tick (✓) the words that describe Dorian Gray.

☐ kind   ☐ selfish   ☐ charming
☐ vain   ☐ ugly   ☐ attractive
☐ clumsy   ☐ cruel
☐ brave   ☐ clever

11 Complete the text about Dorian Gray. Use the given words.

old   evil   kind   ugly
good-looking   selfish   young

At the beginning of the story, Lord Henry Wotton's aunt describes Dorian Gray as serious and ⓐ _____. Lord Henry teaches him to value his youth and beauty and Dorian becomes very vain and ⓑ _____. He decides that youth and beauty are the only things worth having. When he sees the finished portrait, he makes a wish: "I wish that I could always be ⓒ _____, and the portrait could grow ⓓ _____. I would give my soul for that."

The years go by and Dorian Gray remains young and ⓔ _____. The portrait grows old and ugly. With every sin that Dorian commits, the smile becomes more ⓕ _____ and the face uglier.

Finally, Dorian decides that the portrait is the only evidence of his sins. He must destroy the portrait. However, when he stabs the portrait, he dies and he becomes old and ⓖ _____. The portrait becomes young and handsome again.

📢 **12** Write a short description of each of the characters.
What do you think of each one? Share with a partner.

DORIAN GRAY

LORD HENRY WOTTON

BASIL HALLWARD

SIBYL VANE

📢 **13** Who says this? Do you agree with them?
Tick (✓), then tell a partner.

a "Love is more important than money." ☐

b "I wish I could stay young and the ☐
portrait grow old."

c "Sin writes itself across a man's face. ☐
You can't hide it."

d "Each of us has heaven and hell in him." ☐

e "You destroyed the life of Sibyl Vane." ☐

f "An artist should create beautiful things, ☐
but he shouldn't put anything of his own
life into them."

D Plot and Theme

14 Complete the sentences about the portrait with the words below. Which one does Basil say?

cruelty   life   good   evil (x2)

change   conscience

a This portrait will guide me through life. It will be my

   _____.

b It holds the secret of my _____, and it tells my story.

c The portrait will never _____.

d The picture has changed. There is a touch of _____ in the mouth.

e If I'm _____, maybe the portrait will become beautiful again.

f There was nothing _____ in my portrait. This is the face of _____.

15 Which sentence in Exercise **14** is untrue?

16 Put the pictures of the portrait into the correct order. Then write a sentence describing each picture.

17 Tick (✓) true (T) or false (F).

T F (a) Dorian Gray leads a bad life so he must be punished.

T F (b) Dorian is selfish. He only cares about himself.

T F (c) Dorian is always kind to his friends.

T F (d) Dorian Gray is beautiful on the outside but not on the inside.

T F (e) Lord Henry Wotton is a good influence on Dorian.

T F (f) James Vane reminds Dorian that he can't get away with his sins forever.

T F (g) Dorian destroys the portrait and continues his life.

P 18 Look at the text. What does it say?

TIRED OF FEELING OLD?

✓ Visit our clinic to bring youth back to your face
✓ Guaranteed youthful appearance
✓ Only five sessions necessary

The advert says:

(a) youth can make you feel tired.

(b) five sessions can make your face look more youthful.

(c) one visit will make you young again.

19 Do you think youth and beauty are important in today's society? Is this negative or positive? Discuss in groups.

🄴 Language

20 Match the adjectives from the novel with their synonyms.

_____ [a] hideous   [1] very bad

_____ [b] miserable   [2] very interested in

_____ [c] extraordinary   [3] very ugly

_____ [d] terrible   [4] sad

_____ [e] fascinated   [5] sure of oneself

_____ [f] confident   [6] amazing

21 Now complete the sentences with adjectives from Exercise **20**.

[a] When Basil saw the portrait in the schoolroom, the face was _____ .

[b] Sibyl was a _____ actress. She wasn't nervous on stage.

[c] Basil was _____ by Dorian Gray. He needed to see him every day.

[d] Sibyl was _____ when Dorian left her. She was heart-broken.

[e] The portrait was _____ . It grew old and Dorian stayed young.

[f] Sibyl acted badly when Basil and Lord Henry came to see the play. Her performance was _____ .

22 Read the sentences and complete the words.

- a Artists paint these of people.   p _ _ _ _ _ _ _ _
- b James Vane pointed this at Dorian Gray.   g _ _
- c Sibyl Vane swallowed some.   p _ _ _ _ _
- d James Vane didn't like his sister working in this place.   t _ _ _ _ _ _

23 Match the everyday expressions from the novel with their meanings.

- 1 It makes me very unhappy.
- 2 You mustn't criticize him.
- 3 You mustn't get involved.
- 4 That's not important.
- 5 You love him very much.
- 6 I'm happy.
- 7 Isn't that enough?
- 8 I've made another decision.

_____ a That doesn't matter.
_____ b I'm glad.
_____ c You're mad about him.
_____ d I can't bear it.
_____ e I've changed my mind.
_____ f You mustn't get mixed up in it.
_____ g You mustn't say anything against him.
_____ h What more do you want?

24 Complete the sentences with the past simple or past passive of the verbs provided.

a The portrait _____ by Basil Hallward. (paint)

b Sir Geoffrey _____ James Vane by mistake. (shoot)

c The lives of all the characters in the novel except for Lord Henry _____ by Dorian Gray. (destroy)

d Sibyl Vane _____ suicide. (commit)

e The portrait _____ never _____ . (exhibit)

f The artist _____ by Dorian Gray. (murder)

g Dorian _____ the portrait with the same knife that killed the artist. (stab)

TEST

P **1** Choose the correct answer 1, 2, 3 or 4.

_____ a Which of the following does NOT describe Dorian at the beginning of the novel?

1 A very handsome man.

2 A charming man.

3 A vain and selfish man.

4 A friendly and sociable man.

_____ b What does Lord Henry teach Dorian to value?

1 His intelligence.

2 His youth and beauty.

3 His talent as an artist.

4 His friendship with Basil.

_____ c At first Dorian is jealous of the portrait because it _____

1 is more beautiful than him.

2 is very well painted.

3 has a nice frame.

4 will never grow old.

_____ d Dorian's sins show in _____

1 his face.   2 the portrait.

3 his eyes.   4 Basil's hands.

_____ e The portrait is Dorian's _____

1 own creation.   2 best friend.

3 best work.   4 conscience.

2 Answer the following questions.

[a] What does Dorian Gray look like?

[b] Why doesn't the artist want to exhibit the painting?

[c] When Dorian Gray sees the portrait, what does he wish for?

[d] Why doesn't Basil Hallward want Lord Henry to meet Dorian?

[e] Which musical instrument can Dorian play?

[f] Who does Dorian Gray fall in love with?

[g] When does Dorian first notice a change in the portrait?

[h] What does he decide to do when he sees the horrible change?

[i] What does Dorian Gray do with the portrait?

[j] Who does Dorian show the portrait to? Why?

[k] Who tries to kill Dorian Gray on the quay?

[l] Why doesn't he kill him?

[m] How do the characters die?

[n] Who kills Dorian Gray?

[o] What happens to the portrait at the end of the story?

3 Look at these two pictures. How are they similar and how are they different? Work with a partner. Ask and answer questions about the two pictures.

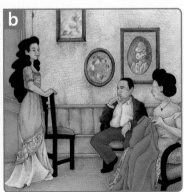

Dorian Gray says in the novel "Each of us has heaven and hell in him." We each have good and evil in us.

Good and evil

Create a poster on the theme of good and evil.

01 Choose five positive words to describe yourself. Then write the opposites.

POSITIVE WORDS	OPPOSITES

02 Now draw two portraits of yourself to show your positive and then your negative characteristics.

Web 03 Use the Internet to find information about *Dr Jekyll and Mr Hyde*. Write a list about the good and evil sides to the main character in this novel.

Web 04 Use the Internet to find a contemporary book with a character who has a good and evil side. Write a description of the character or characters.

作者簡介

1854 年，奧斯卡‧王爾德（Oscar Wilde）出生於愛爾蘭的都柏林，是知名的劇作家、小說家、詩人和幽默家。他一共有九本戲劇作品，最有名的劇作是《不可兒戲》。《道林‧格雷的畫像》是他生平唯一一部小說。他也創作一些童話故事，如《快樂王子與其他故事》，但他表示這些故事不是為兒童而寫，而是為「具有童心的大人」所作。

王爾德的父親威廉‧王爾德爵士是知名的眼科醫師，母親珍‧懷爾德是作家。王爾德在學校時，希臘文和拉丁文表現優異。他先是拿到愛爾蘭都柏林學院攻讀古典文學的獎學金，後來又拿到英格蘭牛津大學的獎學金。王爾德畢業之後，移居倫敦，和一位受歡迎的肖像畫畫家友人法蘭克‧邁爾斯同住。1881 年，他出版了第一本詩集。

1882 年，王爾德搭船前往紐約，展開在美國的巡迴演講。他抵達時，對紐約的海關官員說了一句有名的話：「我無可申報，除了我的才情。」透過家具的選用和穿著，他演說了家居裝潢美學的重要性。

1884 年，王爾德和康絲坦斯‧羅伊德結婚，育有二子。1887 年，他擔任新發行的時尚雜誌月刊《女性世界》的編輯。王爾德繼續創作，他的諸多作品震撼了當時維多利亞時代的社會，但仍廣受歡迎。王爾德雖然功成名就，在 1890 年代卻飽受醜聞的困擾。1895 年，他遭到逮捕，入獄兩年。1900 年，奧斯卡‧王爾德在潦倒中離開人世。

李書簡介

《道林·格雷的畫像》是一部哥德式的恐怖小說（見第 12 頁第八大題），是奧斯卡·王爾德唯一一部問世的小說。1890 年，這部小說首次出刊登於月刊上時，即受到撻伐。王爾德後來作了大幅的改寫，新改寫的故事於 1891 年以小說的形式發行，但再次招致批評，在當時並引發了王爾德的醜聞。王爾德的夫人康絲坦斯曾說：「打從奧斯卡寫了《道林·格雷》之後，就沒有人要跟我們打交道了。」知名書店 W.H. Smiths 拒賣這本書，不過儘管飽受爭議，這本書仍然暢銷。

奧斯卡·王爾德是一位成功的劇作家，《道林·格雷的畫像》的寫作風格更像戲劇而非小說，小說的對白多於敘述，並集中於三位主要人物之間的機智對話：藝術家貝佐·哈霍、富裕友人亨利·沃頓勳爵，和俊美青年道林·格雷。

崇尚美和享樂的這種空虛，是小說主要的主題之一。亨利·沃頓勳爵在小說中說，人生應該為美和享樂而活，而不是為責任而活。他慫恿道林·格雷享受自己的人生，並跟道林說應該趁青春和美貌消逝之前，盡情享受。道林·格雷聽了他的話，過著自私放蕩的生活。在結尾時，他明白到自己的錯誤，卻為時已晚，他已經毀滅了自己的靈魂。

這部小說至今仍受到歡迎，已有十三部改編的影片。2007 年，漫威漫畫公司出版了這部小說的漫畫改編版本。

Chapter 1

P.15

　　畫室裡瀰漫著一股芬芳的花香，夏日的輕風拂過花園裡的樹木，從敞開的門吹進來。亨利・沃頓勳爵這時正躺在睡椅上。

　　在房間的中央，有一幅美如潘安的年輕人肖像畫。畫像前，坐著藝術家貝佐・哈霍。

　　「貝佐，這是你最好的作品了，你一定要把它送去畫廊。」亨利勳爵說道。

　　「我哪裡都不送。」貝佐回答。

　　亨利勳爵用詫異的眼神望著他：「哪裡都不送？是怎麼著，老兄？」

　　「我知道你會笑我，不過這幅畫不能送展，畫裡頭有太多的『我』了。」貝佐回答。

　　亨利勳爵笑道：「畫裡頭有太多的『你』？畫裡頭的人根本不像你！你的臉

那麼粗獷，頭髮黑得像煤炭，可是畫中的年輕人可是用象牙和玫瑰花瓣做成的，我敢說他不會思考，是個沒大腦的漂亮男孩。你根本不像他啦。」

　　「你不了解我，亨利。不過當然啦，我的外表是長得不像道林・格雷。」貝佐回答。

P.16

　　「道林・格雷？這是他的名字？」亨利勳爵問。

　　「對，是他的名字。我本來不想說的。」

　　「幹嘛不跟我說？」

　　「我也說不上來。只要是我喜歡的人，他們的名字我都不會跟人家講的。我喜歡保密，這樣可以給現代生活添些神祕感。我猜你會覺得我很蠢吧。」

　　亨利勳爵笑了笑，掏出懷錶，說道：「貝佐，我該走啦。不過在我離開之前，你要問答我一個問題。」

　　「什麼問題？」貝佐問。

　　「你為什麼不將道林・格雷的畫像送展？跟我說真正的原因吧。」

P.17

　　「每一幅用感情去畫出來的肖像畫，畫的其實不是模特兒，而是藝術家自己。我不想把這幅畫送展，是因為我不想暴露我心底的祕密。」

　　亨利勳爵笑著問道：「什麼祕密？」

　　「兩個月前，我去參加布蘭登夫人的宴會。去了十分鐘左右，正當我和打扮浮華的貴婦以及無趣的教授們談話時，我突然感覺到有人在打量我。我側身望過

去，這是我第一次見到道林‧格雷。我們眼神一交會，我便蒼白失色了，我感到我的生命將遭遇一次可怕的危難。

P.18

我感到害怕，轉身想離開房間。我快步走向門口，卻撞見了布蘭登夫人。她把我又拉回宴會上，這時我發現自己眼前所面對的竟然就是那位年輕人。於是我請布蘭登夫人把我介紹給他認識。」

「那麼布蘭登夫人是怎麼形容那位奇妙的年輕人的？」亨利勳爵問。

「哦，她是這樣說的，『漂亮男孩——我不記得他是做什麼的——也可能沒在做什麼——哦，對了，他在彈鋼琴——還是在拉小提琴呢，親愛的格雷先生？』我們不禁都笑了出來，頓時交上了朋友。」

「笑容，是一段友誼的美好開始，也是最好的結束。」亨利勳爵說。

「貝佐，再跟我說說道林‧格雷先生的事吧。你們多久見一次面？」亨利勳爵繼續說道。

「每天都見面。我非得每天見他不可。」

「我還以為你只對自己的藝術有興趣。」

「現在對我來說，他就是我的藝術。我遇到道林‧格雷之後所畫的創作，是我這一生最好的作品。」貝佐說。

「貝佐，這可神奇了，我一定要見見道林‧格雷這個人。」

貝佐從坐椅上站起來，在房間裡回來踱著步。他思索了半晌後，說道：「亨利，道林‧格雷帶給我靈感，但你從他身上可能看不到什麼。」

「那你為什麼就不把他的肖像畫送展？」亨利勳爵問。

「我不想向世人暴露我的內心。」

P.19

「詩人就不會像你這樣，他們知道破碎的心很暢銷。」

「我討厭他們這樣。藝術家是要創作美好的事物，而不是把自己生活中的東西放進去。時下，人們把藝術當成是一種自傳的形式，失去了美的抽象意義。所以說，世人將看不到我畫的道林‧格雷肖像。」貝佐叫道。

藝術

- 你覺得呢？藝術是要像自傳，還是只能單純的表現美？
- 你想得到有什麼自傳性藝術的例子嗎？請分組討論。

「貝佐，我想你錯囉。」亨利勳爵說著，又補充道：「老兄，我想起來了！」

「想起什麼，亨利？」

「我在什麼地方聽過道林·格雷這個名字。」

「什麼地方？」貝佐蹙眉問道。

「貝佐，你別這樣一臉怒氣。是在我姑媽愛葛莎夫人的家裡啦。她跟我說有一個優異的年輕人，在東區幫忙她打理事情，她說那個人的名字叫作道林·格雷。她說他很認真、很親切。」

「亨利，我不想讓你和他碰面。」

就在這時，管家走了進來。

「先生，道林·格雷先生在大廳裡了。」管家說。

「這下子你不介紹一下也不行啦。」亨利勳爵叫著笑了起來。

貝佐看著亨利勳爵，說道：「道林·格雷是我最親愛的朋友，你姑媽說的是對的，你可不要把他帶壞了。你不要想去影響他，那準沒好事。」

亨利勳爵笑道：「真是胡說八道！」然後對管家說：「帶他進來吧。」

不好的影響

- 你覺得人們或朋友之間會互相影響好壞嗎？會如何影響呢？和夥伴討論看看。

Chapter 2

「貝佐，我姿勢擺膩了，而且我不想要一個真人尺寸的畫像。」敞開的門外傳來的聲音說道。

這時，道林·格雷走進了房間。當他看到亨利勳爵時，露出一臉尷尬。「抱歉，貝佐，我不知道你有訪客。」

「道林，這是亨利·沃頓勳爵，一位朋友。」貝佐說。

「很高興認識你！」亨利勳爵說：「我的愛葛莎姑媽常跟我提到你，你是她特別喜歡的人。」

「我現在被列在愛葛莎夫人的黑名單上了，」道林回答說：「上星期二，我答應陪她去白教堂區的一家俱樂部，可是我卻忘得一乾二淨，她找我和她表演鋼琴雙人合奏。」

「我想你沒去也不是什麼大不了的事，搞不好聽眾會以為她就是在表演合奏，愛葛莎姑媽一彈起琴來，吵得就像雙人合奏一樣。」亨利勳爵說。

「你真壞。」道林笑著回答道。

亨利勳爵看看道林，他確實長得很帥，紅唇，藍眼，金髮。

貝佐把顏料拌好，準備好畫筆，一臉憂心的樣子。

「亨利，我想在今天把畫完成，可以請你離開了嗎？」他說。

亨利勳爵露出微笑，看著道林·格雷問道：「格雷先生，我要走嗎？」

「哦，請不要走。」

「那好，我就留下來。貝佐，你不會真的介意吧？你不是喜歡你的姊姊們有聊天的伴嗎！」

「如果道林希望你留下來，那你當然就得留下來。」貝佐說。

「道林，現在走上臺子吧。別聽亨利勳爵的話就是了，他的朋友都被他帶壞了，除了我以外。」

貝佐一邊畫著，亨利勳爵就在一旁和道林閒聊。道林‧格雷這時突然大聲說道：「貝佐，我站累了。我要出去，去花園裡坐坐，裡面太悶了。」

「我和你一起去花園。」亨利勳爵說。

「別讓道林待太久，我想把這幅畫完成。這將會成為我的代表作。」

亨利勳爵和道林走出了門，進到花園裡，說道：「我們坐在樹蔭下，你一定不想曬傷吧！」

P.24

「無所謂啦。」道林笑著叫道。

「格雷先生，這可有所謂了。」

「怎麼說？」

「你還年輕啊，青春要好好把握。」

「這我倒不覺得，亨利勳爵。」

「你現在是不覺得，等你有一天老了、皺了、醜了，你就有感啦。你在笑？等你青春一去不復返，就笑不出來啦。青春一消逝，美貌也會隨之消逝。趁著青春時，好好享受吧！不要把你的黃金歲月浪費在幫助病人和窮人上面。去活出你的生命吧！花謝了，會有再開的時候，青春一去就不復返了。」

青春

• 寫出和青春有關的五樣東西，好的壞的都可以寫，然後和朋友分享。

這時，畫室的門口突然現出貝佐的身影，他喊道：「我在等著，請進來吧，現在的光線很剛好。」

P.26

他們一起沿著小徑走，「認識我，你開心嗎，格雷先生？」亨利勳爵看著他問道。

「當然，我現在很開心，但我應該都要一直很開心嗎？」

「一直？這是可怕的字眼，女人特別愛這兩個字，她們努力要讓浪漫永久持續下去，反倒因此毀掉了每一次的浪漫。」

他們走進畫室，道林‧格雷又走上了臺子。亨利勳爵坐在大扶椅上看著他。

一刻鐘之後，貝佐停下畫筆，喊道：「完成了！」

接著，他在畫布的左邊角落裡，寫上瘦長的朱紅色字落款。

道林看著自己的肖畫像，他這時才第一次意識到自己的美貌。「現在我明白亨利勳爵那番話的意思了。沒錯，有一天，我的臉會皺掉，變得又老又醜。」一想到這裡，他感到一陣如刀刺般的劇痛。

「你不喜歡嗎？」貝佐叫道。

「他當然喜歡啊，畫得太好啦，賣給我吧！」亨利勳爵說。

「這並不屬於我，亨利。」

「那是屬於誰的？」

「當然是道林的。」貝佐回答。

P. 27

「他真幸運了。」亨利勳爵說。

道林‧格雷說道：「太悲哀了！我會變老變醜，畫像卻會永遠年輕，將來都不會比今天這個樣子老。真希望可以相反過來，讓我可以永保青春，而讓畫像去變老！我願意拿靈魂來作交換。亨利‧沃頓勳爵說得沒錯，青春是唯一值得擁有的東西。等我發現自己老了，我會自我了斷。」

貝佐的臉色頓時發白。「道林，不要說這種話！」他叫道。

「你在乎的是什麼，貝佐？對你來說，你的藝術比你的朋友重要。我妒嫉這幅畫，哦，你何苦畫它呢？」道林問道。

願望

‧道林的願望是什麼？把它寫下來。

「亨利，這是你的錯！我不會讓這幅畫破壞了我們的感情。」貝佐生氣地說道。

道林看著貝佐朝窗戶邊的桌子走過去，他在找調色刀。他找到了。

P. 29

「他要把畫布毀掉！」道林心想。他跑向貝佐，搶下貝佐手上的刀，扔到畫室的另一頭。「不要，貝佐！這是謀殺！」他叫道。

「我很開心你總算是欣賞我的畫，道林。」貝佐說。

「貝佐，我很喜歡這幅畫，它是我的一部分。」

「好吧，等你一乾了，我就把你裱框起來，然後送你回家。之後，你想怎麼處置自己，就怎麼處置吧。」這時傳來敲門聲，管家端著茶走進來。

「我們今晚去劇院看戲吧！」亨利勳爵說。

「我想跟你一起去，亨利勳爵。」道林說。

「你呢，貝佐？」

「我不能去，我還有很多事情要處理。」

「那麼，格雷先生，就我們兩個一起去囉。」

「我太高興了。」道林説。

貝佐蹙著眉頭，走到畫像旁，傷心地説：「我會和真實的道林待在一起。」

「它是真的道林嗎？我真的像他嗎？」年輕人叫道。

「是的，一模一樣。」貝佐説。

「太神奇了，貝佐！」

「至少你的外表和畫像是一樣的。」貝佐嘆息道：「畫像永遠不會改變，價值就在這裡。」

Chapter 3

P. 30

一個月後，某個下午，道林・格雷坐在亨利勳爵位於梅費爾區家中小圖書室的扶手椅上。

「永遠不要結婚！男人結婚，是因為累了；女人結婚，是出於好奇。最後雙方都失望了。」亨利勳爵説。

「我想我不會結婚，亨利，我陷入愛太深了。」

「你愛上誰？」亨利勳爵問。

「一個女演員，她叫希貝兒・魏恩。」道林・格雷説。

「我沒聽説過這個人。」

「沒有人聽過，不過有一天會的。她很出色。」

「你認識她多久了？」

「大概三個星期。」

「在哪裡認識？」

「有一天晚上，我決定外出去探險一下。我發現了一家奇怪的小劇院，決定走進去探探究竟。那齣戲是《羅密歐與茱麗葉》。那地方糟透了，不過我決定還是看完第一幕。羅密歐是個又矮又胖的老男人，莫古修也差不多糟，但茱麗葉！她是我這輩子看過最可愛的女孩。她十七歲左右，有著像花一樣的小臉蛋，深色的波浪秀髮，紫羅蘭色的眼眸，玫瑰花瓣的嘴唇，而她的聲音——我從來沒聽過這麼美妙的聲音……」道林停頓了下來。

P. 31

「亨利，我愛她。」他繼續説道：「夜復一夜，我都去看她表演。女演員太美好了，女演員就是不一樣。」

「亨利，你怎麼沒有告訴我，唯一值得去愛的就是女演員。」道林説。

「因為我愛過太多個了，道林。」亨利勳爵回答。

「那我現在後悔跟你説希貝兒・魏恩的事了。」

「道林，你要跟我説，你這輩子所做的事都要告訴我。」

「沒錯，這倒是真的。你對我有一種奇怪的影響力。就算我犯罪，我也會告訴你。」

「道林，像你這樣的人才不會犯罪。現在告訴我，你們認識了嗎？」

「當然。我第三天晚上就去見她了。那天她演羅莎琳，我丟了一些花到臺上，她望向我。當晚，有個老人提議説要帶我去後臺，所以我就去了。我們兩

個都很緊張。那個老人一直叫我『閣下大人』。我告訴希貝兒，我才不是什麼大人。她卻說：『你看起來更像個王子，我要叫你白馬王子。』喔，亨利！我每晚都去看她演出，每晚，她愈加出色了。」

P.33

「所以，這就是你現在都不跟我共進晚餐的原因囉。我想你一定是戀愛了。道林，你今晚可以跟我一起用餐吧，還是說不行呢？」

他搖搖頭。

「亨利，我要你和貝佐一起來看她演戲。我知道你們兩個會愛上她的。然後我們要帶她離開劇院。她還要為那個老人工作三年，所以當然我得付他一些錢。等一切都處理好了，我會幫她在倫敦西區找個劇院。她會讓全世界都為她癡迷的，就像她讓我為她癡迷一樣。」

「那是不可能的，親愛的孩子。」

「會，一定會的。」

「好吧，那我們什麼時候去？」亨利勳爵問。

「明天就去吧，她明天演茱麗葉。」道林回答。

「好吧。那你要通知貝佐，還是我來寫信給他？」

「親愛的貝佐！我一個星期沒見到他了。我真糟糕。他把我的畫像裱上了很美的框，送來給我了。我有點妒嫉那幅畫裡的自己，因為它比我年輕了一個月，不過我還是很喜歡。也許應該由你寫信給他，我不想單獨見他，他會說讓我惱火的話，忠言逆耳。」

P.34

貝佐

• 為什麼道林不再和貝佐那麼交好了？
• 貝佐為什麼會惹惱道林？

道林・格雷在手帕上灑了些香水，說道：「我現在得走了，不要忘了明天，再見。」

當天晚上十二點半左右，當亨利勳爵回到家時，他看到大廳桌上有封電報，那是道林・格雷寄來的，上面寫著：「我準備和希貝兒・魏恩結婚了。」

電報公司

收信人：亨利・沃頓勳爵
寄信人：道林・格雷

我準備和希貝兒・魏恩結婚了。

Chapter 4

P. 35

「媽媽，我太開心了！」女孩輕聲地說：「您一定也很開心！」

魏恩太太看起來很沮喪。「開心！」她重複說道：「希貝兒，我只有看著你演戲時才會開心啊。除了演戲，你什麼都不該多想。艾薩克先生一直對我們很好，而且我們還欠他錢啊。」

「媽媽，錢？」女孩大聲說道：「錢有什麼所謂？愛情比錢重要多了。」

「艾薩克先生給了我們五十磅，讓我們還清債務。希貝兒，這件事你不能忘了。五十磅是一筆很大的數目。艾薩克先生的人很好的。」

希貝兒說：「媽媽，我們不再需要他了，我們現在有白馬王子了。」她停頓了一下，說道：「我愛他。」

「傻孩子！」母親說。女孩又笑了。

母親接著說：「這個年輕人可能很有錢。如果他有錢，你就應該嫁給她。但你還太年輕，還不適合談戀愛。還有，你對他一無所知。甚至連他的名字都不知道，我很擔心。另外你弟弟就要遠赴澳洲了，這讓我很難過。」

P. 36

就在此時，門打開了，一個棕髮的年輕男子走了進來。詹姆士·魏恩很高大，他手腳粗大，動作笨拙，不像姊姊那麼有氣質。魏恩太太看著他，露出微笑。

「喔，詹姆士。」希貝兒叫道。她跑過整個房間上前抱住他。

詹姆士·魏恩滿懷愛意地看著姊姊的臉。「跟我去散散步吧，希貝兒。我想我再也看不到這討厭的倫敦了。」

「兒子啊，別這樣說。等你賺了錢，你就會離開澳洲，回到倫敦。」魏恩太太說。

「我想賺些錢帶你跟希貝兒離開舞臺。我討厭你們這樣。」

希貝兒笑著說道：「喔，詹姆士，你還真不客氣！不過你真的想要跟我去散步嗎？我們去公園吧。」

他說：「好。不過你換衣服可別換太久。」

希貝兒輕快地跳出房門，他可以聽到她上樓時邊哼著歌。他在房裡來回踱了兩三趟，然後轉向母親，問道：「我的東西都準備好了嗎？」

「都準備好了，詹姆士，我希望你在船上的生活一切順心。」她答道。

P. 38

「我聽説有位男士每晚都到劇院，而且還到後臺跟希貝兒説話，真是這樣嗎？」詹姆士問道。

「當戲子的，就是會吸引很多人的注目。我以前有一段時間也收過很多花。至於希貝兒的那位年輕人，他是個優秀的男士。他對我總是彬彬有禮，他送的花也很美。」

「但是，您連他的名字都不知道。」詹姆士生氣地説。

「不，他只是還沒有告訴我他的真名。我覺得他這樣很浪漫啊，他可能是個貴族。」母親回答。

詹姆士·魏恩皺起眉頭，「請看顧好希貝兒，母親。」他大聲地説。

「我一直都有好好地照顧希貝兒。那位男士可能很有錢，這對希貝兒來説可能是個好姻緣。」

就在這時，門打開了，希貝兒跑了進來。「你們兩個好嚴肅喔！」她大聲喊道：「怎麼了？」

「沒事，我們有時候還是得嚴肅一點。母親，一切都打包好了，我晚點回來再好好地道別吧。」詹姆士回答。

「希貝兒，我們走吧。」她弟弟沒耐性地説。

他們出門，沿著陰鬱的尤斯頓路走。希貝兒聊著大船和詹姆士在澳洲的新生活。

詹姆士聽著。對於離家，他很擔心，但最擔心的還是希貝兒。她需要被保護。這個白馬王子對她不懷好意。母親膚淺又愛慕虛榮，她保護不了希貝兒的。此外，他還有件事情想問母親，因為他有天晚上在劇院聽到有人在講她的閒言流語。他皺起了眉頭。

P. 39

「詹姆士，你沒有在聽我説話！」希貝兒喊道：「我在幫你規畫最美好的未來耶，説句話吧。」

「我聽説你交了新朋友了，他是誰？你怎麼都沒有跟我提過他？他對你不懷好意。」

「詹姆士，別説了！」她驚呼道：「你不可以説任何批評的話。我愛他。」

「但是你甚至連他的名字都不知道！他是誰？我想知道。」詹姆士答道。

「他叫白馬王子。等你以後從澳洲回來，終有一天會見到他的，我知道你會喜歡他的。每一個人都喜歡他，而我愛他。我希望你今晚能來劇院，他也會來，我今晚會演茱麗葉。詹姆士，想像一下，陷入愛河的我演出茱麗葉啊！」

「他是紳士。」詹姆士説。

「他是王子！」她喊道：「你還想要什麼？」

「我要你小心他。」

「我見到他，就崇拜他。」

「希貝兒，你被他迷倒了。」

P. 41

她笑著挽起他的手臂。「你要為我高興。生命一直對我們兩個人都很嚴苛，但現在不一樣了，你要去一個新的世界，而我也發現了新的世界。」

「他要是傷害你，我就宰了他。」詹姆士説。

希貝兒害怕地看著他。他又講了一遍同樣的話，那些話像匕首一樣劃破空中，旁人都盯著他們看。

「我們走吧，詹姆士。」希貝兒輕聲說。

他便跟著她穿過人群。

他們在大理石拱門前搭了一輛公共馬車，載著他們駛向位於尤斯頓路上的簡陋家中。

這時已經過了五點，希貝兒在演出前要躺下來休息幾個小時。她向弟弟道別，弟弟走下樓時，他的眼中含著淚水。

當他下樓時，母親正等著他，兩人的眼神交會。

「母親，在離開前，我有件事想問您。」他說：「告訴我實話，您與父親有結婚嗎？」

魏恩太太知道這個問題無可迴避，她答道：「沒有。」

「那我的父親是個爛人。」詹姆士大聲說。

P. 42

她搖搖頭，「我知道他已婚，但我們彼此深愛。如果他現在還活著，他會照顧我們的。別說他的不是，兒子。他是你的父親，他是個紳士。」

詹姆士很生氣，「希貝兒現在的對象也是個紳士，不是嗎？」

母親用顫抖的雙手，拭去自己眼裡的淚水，說道：「希貝兒還有個媽媽，而我卻沒有。」

詹姆士一時動容，便走向母親，彎下腰來親吻她，說道：「對不起，我現在得走了。相信我，這個男人如果敢做出任何傷害姊姊的事情，我會把他揪出來，宰了他。我發誓。」

之後詹姆士得趕去搭船，當他離開時，母親從窗邊向他揮手道別。

保護

• 你認為詹姆士保護自己的姊姊是對的嗎？

• 你有沒有要保護的兄弟姊妹或朋友？和朋友討論看看。

Chapter 5

P.43

「貝佐，我猜你聽到了風聲。」當晚亨利勳爵在晚餐時說。

「沒有，亨利。什麼事？」貝佐回答。

「道林・格雷準備要結婚了。」亨利勳爵說

貝佐皺起眉頭，「不可能。」

「千真萬確。」

「跟誰？」

「跟一個小演員。」

「可是想想道林的地位和財富，他不能跟女演員結婚。」

「你要是這樣跟他說，那他就娶她娶定了。」

「我希望那女孩是個好人家，亨利。」

「道林說她很漂亮，我們今晚就看得到她了。」

「但是你贊成嗎，亨利？」貝佐問。

「你知道我不是婚姻的擁護者。我希望道林・格雷娶這個女孩，瘋狂地愛戀她六個月，然後又突然琵琶別抱。」

「你不是當真的吧，亨利。」

亨利勳爵笑道：「我當然是說真的啦。不過道林來了。」

「親愛的亨利，親愛的貝佐，你們兩位得恭喜我了，我從沒有這麼開心過。來吧，我們到劇院去。」道林說。

P.44

婚姻

• 道林的朋友對他與希貝兒的未來婚姻看法如何？
• 你覺得這是個好跡象嗎？

那天晚上劇院擠滿了人，而且又很熱。

「這真是個和愛人相見的好地方啊！」亨利勳爵說。

「別擔心！等希貝兒上場時，你就什麼都忘掉了。」道林說。

一刻鐘後，在熱烈掌聲中，希貝兒・魏恩上臺了。的確，她看起來很可人。

「是我見過最可愛的女孩之一。」亨利勳爵心想。

貝佐・哈霍站起來開始鼓掌。道林・格雷坐著凝視著她。希貝兒・魏恩很美，卻意外地毫無感情。她扮演茱麗葉，在看到羅密歐時，臉上卻看不到喜悅的表情，而且說話的樣子很不自然。

道林・格雷看著她，臉色都發白了。他感到疑惑，也很擔心。他的兩個朋友什麼也沒說。那女孩不會演戲，他們都很失望。而這不是怯場，她很有自信，純粹就是演得不好，觀眾看得也興味索然，開始大聲喧嘩，吹起口哨來。

P.46

亨利勳爵從座位上起身，披上外套，說道：「道林，她是很美，但是不會演戲。我們走吧。」

「我要把戲看完。」道林用苦澀的語氣回答。

「親愛的道林，我想衛恩小姐一定是生病了，我們改天晚上再來。」貝佐說。「希望她只是生病了，但我看她還好。她變了。昨天晚上她還是個很優異的演員，今天晚上卻演得很走樣。」道林說。

「我們走吧，親愛的孩子，別看起來那麼哀戚！希貝兒・魏恩很美，你還奢望什麼？」亨利勳爵說。

「走開，亨利，我想獨處一下。」道林說：「你沒見到我的心都碎了嗎？」他把臉埋在手裡。

「我們走吧，貝佐。」亨利勳爵說。這兩個人於是一起離開。

表演一結束，道林‧格雷就跑到後臺的更衣室。女孩獨自站著，臉上帶著勝利的表情。當他進來時，她對他微笑道，「道林，我今天晚上的演出很糟！」她開心地大叫。

「糟透了！」他驚訝地瞪著她回答：「慘不忍睹。」

女孩笑著回答道：「道林，難道你不懂嗎？」

「懂什麼？」他生氣地問。

「我今天晚上為什麼會表現得這麼走樣。」

P.47

他聳聳肩，「我猜你是生病了。生病了，就不應該上臺。」

她沒有聽進他講什麼話，她太開心了，直說道：「道林，今天晚上是我有生以來的第一次看透了劇院的愚蠢，我看到羅密歐又醜又老，還化了大濃妝。果園裡的月光是假的，我得說的臺詞也是假的，那些都不是我真心想說的。你讓我了解到愛情的真正樣子。我的愛人！白馬王子！生命中的王子！我厭倦表演了。今晚當我出場時，我想好好表現一番，可是我卻發現我演不下去。我聽到他們說話，我笑了。他們哪懂什麼是愛？道林，帶我走吧，我討厭舞臺，我再也演不下去了。戀愛的戲我演不出來，我就是在戀愛中啊！」

道林跌坐在沙發上，說道：「你扼殺了我的愛。」

她走過來，輕觸他的頭髮，他卻跳起來走到門邊，「一旦你褪去才華，就什麼都不是了。我本想讓你揚名立萬的，讓全世界的人都愛慕你。我本想要你嫁給我的，但你現在是什麼？一個有著漂亮臉蛋的爛演員。我再也不要見到你了。」

希貝兒臉色發白，說道：「道林，你不是認真的吧？你在演戲。」

P.48

「演戲？那是你的份，你演得可好了。」他無情地回應。

她穿過整個房間跑向他，把手放在他的手臂上，直視著他的眼睛。

「別碰我！」他大喊。

「道林，不要離開我！我承受不住的！」她輕聲地說：「你就不能原諒今晚的事嗎？我也只是演壞了這一次。噢，請不要離開我！」

P. 49

她痛哭了起來。道林用鄙夷的眼神看著她，她的眼淚讓他更不耐煩了。最後，他用沉著的聲音說：「我走了，我不想這麼無情，但我沒辦法再見你。你讓我太失望了。」

她靜靜地啜泣著，未發一語。他離開了更衣室。

鄙視

· 從這裡，我們看到了道林個性中不同的哪一面？

· 你怎麼看待道林的反應？和朋友討論看看。

不一會兒，道林走出了劇院。他在黯淡的街上徘徊，路過黑影籠罩的門和面目猙獰的房子。黎明破曉時，他招手攬了一輛馬車載他回家。

到家時，他脫下帽子和外套，穿過書房往臥室的門走去。當他轉動門把，看到那幅肖像畫時，吃了一驚。他走近肖像畫，仔細瞧了瞧。

肖像畫的表情看起來不一樣，嘴角邊竟然出現了幾道殘酷的線條，太奇怪了。

P. 51

他從桌上拿起一面鏡子，他的嘴唇並沒有什麼紋路啊。這代表了什麼？他又再度仔細端詳那幅畫，毫無疑問，表情的確是不同了。他坐下來思索著。

突然間，他想到畫像完成那天，他在貝佐·哈霍的畫室裡心中所起過的念頭，「我希望我能永保青春，讓肖像去變老；我要我的美貌永遠不變，讓畫布上的面容去改變就好；我想要維持住青春的美好，莫非是我的願望實現了？不可能啊，不過肖像畫的確是變了，無疑的嘴角出現了一抹殘酷無情的筆觸。無情！我無情嗎？是那女孩的錯，不是我，是她讓我太失望了。」

這時，他記起她像個小孩般倒臥在他腳邊啜泣的樣子。「我對她太無情了，真是不可原諒。可是，我也不好受啊。我為什麼就該擔心希貝兒·魏恩？」

之後他看著帶著殘酷笑容的肖像，「它已經變了。我每造一次孽，就會出現一個印記，來破壞它的美。但是我不會再造孽了，我要跟希貝兒道歉，然後娶她。我對她的愛會再回來的。」

Chapter 6

P.52

　當道林起床時，已經過了中午。昨晚的悲劇就像一場夢。他換好衣服後，走到書房坐下來吃早餐。他收到一封亨利勳爵的信，但是他決定不打開來看。這是美好的一天，他覺得很開心。當他看到畫像前的屏風時，便跳起身起來。

　道林很快地起身，鎖上兩側的門，然後拉開屏風，盯著那張臉瞧。

　的的確確，肖像已經變了。

　「好的是它讓我看到自己對待希貝兒·魏恩是如何的殘忍，去跟她道歉還不算太晚，她還是會作我的妻子。這幅肖像畫可以引領我一輩子，它會是我的良心寫照。」他想。

　時鐘敲了三點鐘，又過了四點，道林·格雷還沒有動靜。

　最後，他坐在桌前，寫了一封熱情洋溢的信要給希貝兒，求她原諒。

良心
- 畫像要如何成為道林的良心寫照？
- 你的良心告訴你要做些什麼？向朋友說明一下。

P.53

　這時，突然傳來一陣敲門聲，門外傳來亨利勳爵的聲音。「親愛的孩子，我得見你一面，讓我進去。」

　他跳起身來，迅速地拉上屏風遮住那幅畫，然後才打開門。

　他從椅子上起身，把畫像前的大屏風拉上，接著走到窗邊，打開窗戶。早晨新鮮的空氣，驅走了他所有黑暗的念頭。

「我很遺憾，道林。」當他進來時說道：「但你千萬別想太多。」

「你是指希貝兒‧魏恩的事嗎？」道林問。

「當然，事情很慘，但這不是你的錯。」亨利勳爵回答：「你在表演結束之後，有去後臺找她？」

「有啊。」

「你跟她吵架了？」

「我對她太狠心了，亨利，但現在沒事了，這讓我更了解自己了。」

「噢，道林，很高興你是這樣看待的！我以為你會很難過。」

道林笑道：「我現在很開心，知道良心是什麼了，我想要做一個好人，我不能忍受自己的靈魂變得邪惡。」

「那太好了！道林，我要恭喜你，那你要從哪裡開始著手呢？」

「娶希貝兒‧魏恩啊。」

P. 54

「娶希貝兒‧魏恩？」亨利勳爵站起身，吃驚地看著他，喊道：「親愛的道林，你沒收到我的信嗎？」

「你的信？喔，對，我記起來了，但我還沒看，亨利。」

「所以你不知道囉？」

「什麼意思？」

猜猜看

‧你認為亨利勳爵在信中說了什麼？

亨利勳爵走過房間，坐到道林‧格雷的身邊，將他的雙手握在自己手中，說道：「道林，別怕。我的信就是要告訴你，希貝兒‧魏恩死了。」

道林口中迸出了一聲痛苦的嘶喊，「死了！希貝兒死了！這不是真的！」

「是真的，道林，今天早上的報紙都刊登了。當然，接下來會有一場死因調查，你千萬不能牽涉其中。劇院的人知道你的名字嗎？如果不知道，那就沒事了。」亨利勳爵說。

道林好一會兒沒回話，他驚嚇得茫茫然。

終於，他說道：「亨利，你說死因調查？難道希貝兒是……？噢，亨利，我承受不住！」

P. 55

「道林，那不是意外。當她和她母親準備離開劇院時，她又上樓回去拿東西。他們等著她，但她卻再也沒下樓來。他們發現她倒臥在更衣室的地上斷氣了。他們認為應該是喝了毒藥。」

「亨利，好悲慘呀！」道林喊道。

「的確，但是你千萬不能牽涉進去。道林，你不可以讓這件事情打擊到你。你晚上跟我一起吃飯，接著我們去看歌劇。我姊姊訂了個包廂。」

「所以希貝兒‧魏恩是我害死的，而小鳥依然在我的花園裡輕快的啼唱著。我今晚會跟你一起吃飯，然後去看歌劇。生活是多麼的戲劇性！噢，亨利，我曾經是那麼愛她！她曾經是我的一切。接著，那個可怕的夜晚到來——真的就是昨晚的事嗎？她演出走樣，然後我就甩了她。」道林說。

「後來，發生了一件讓我害怕的事。」

道林繼續説道:「我決定回到她身邊,她卻死了。天啊!亨利,我該怎麼辦?你不懂我身處的危險。現在我已經用不著做個正人君子了。」

P.56

「親愛的道林,你比我走運,我還沒有心愛的女人是為我而死的。」亨利勳爵回答。

「別忘了,是我對希貝兒太狠心了。」

接下來是一陣沉默。房間裡暗了下來,暗影從花園潛入。

一會兒後,道林·格雷抬起頭來,「就別再聊我的感情了。那是一段奇妙的經歷,就只是這樣。」

「我們現在去俱樂部吃飯吧。已經晚了。」亨利勳爵説。

「我會去劇院找你,亨利。我現在很累,什麼都吃不下。你姊姊的包廂是幾號?」

「二十七號。門上會有她的名字。」

「謝謝你告訴我這一切,你是我最好的朋友。」道林説。

「我們的友誼才剛開始呢,道林。那我走了,待會見。」亨利勳爵回答道。

黑暗
• 找出黑暗和黑影的比喻,你想那代表著什麼?

Chapter 7

P.57

隔天早上,道林在吃早餐時,貝佐·哈霍被領進了屋裡。

「道林,很高興我找到你了。我昨天晚上來找你,他們説你去看歌劇了。當然我知道這是不可能的。我在報紙上看到了希貝兒的死訊,就立刻趕過來了。我知道你一定很痛苦。你去哪裡了?你有去找那女孩的母親嗎?可憐的女人!她一定很難過!她對這一切説了什麼嗎?」貝佐説。

「親愛的貝佐,我怎麼會知道?我去看歌劇了。我第一次見到關杜蘭夫人,亨利的姊姊。我們待在她的包廂裡。她真是迷人啊。」道林説。

127

「你去看歌劇了？」貝佐吃驚地說：「希貝兒倒在地上死掉時，你去看了歌劇？你心愛的女孩死了，你竟然跟我說別的女人有多迷人？」

「別說了，貝佐！我不想聽！現在一切都已經過去了。」道林說。

「你說昨天是過去？道林，這太可怕了！什麼東西改變了你，你說話的樣子，就像個沒有心肝的人。都是亨利影響了你。我這陣子都沒看到你。你要再來讓我畫。」

「我不會再讓你畫了，貝佐。」道林大聲說。

P. 59

貝佐張大眼睛看著他，問道：「為什麼不要？你不喜歡我幫你畫的肖像嗎？畫放在哪？你為什麼用屏風把它遮住？我要看一下。道林，把屏風拿開，我要看看那幅畫像。」

「不可以！」道林用驚恐的聲音喊道，然後跑到貝佐和屏風之間。「你不可以看。」

「我為什麼不能看那幅畫？」貝佐笑著問。

「貝佐，你要是看了，我就永遠不跟你講話了。」

貝佐驚訝地看著道林，「我打算秋天時在巴黎展出。」

道林很害怕，喊道：「你說過你不想送展的，你怎麼變卦了？為什麼你之前不想展出我的畫像？」

貝佐露出愁容，「你注意到這幅畫有什麼奇怪的地方了嗎？」

「貝佐！」道林用著恐懼的眼神喊道。

「不用說了，我明白，道林。從我認識你的那一刻起，你的個性就對我產生了一種奇怪的影響。然後就在命中註定的那天，我決定畫下你的肖像。我把一切都注入那幅畫中。道林，後來我覺得那幅畫中有太多的自我了，所以我決定永遠不送展。幾天後，那幅畫離開了我的工作室之後，我感覺一切都只是我的想像罷了，它就只是一幅很出色的畫而已。你長得很帥，而我是個好畫家。所以當我收到巴黎寄來的邀約時，我就決定要在我的畫展中展出你的肖像畫。不過，你是對的，不會將它送展的。」

P. 60

道林露出了笑容。危險告終，他此刻算是安全了。

「我現在可以看那幅畫了嗎？」貝佐問。

道林搖搖頭。

「好吧，也許你是對的。我現在得走了。」

在他走出房間後，道林對自己笑著說：「可憐的貝佐！他不知道真正的原因！」他嘆了口氣，搖了鈴，「我一定要把這幅畫藏起來，不讓任何人看到。」他想。

管家黎夫太太走了進來，道林跟她要了書房的鑰匙。

「道林先生，是那間舊書房嗎？但裡面都是灰塵，已經有五年沒有人進去過了。」她叫喊著說。

「沒關係，我只是想看看那地方，就這樣而已。把鑰匙給我。」道林答道。

「先生，鑰匙在這裡。」老婦人說。

「謝謝你，黎夫太太。現在沒事了。」

門一關上，道林就把鑰匙放進口袋，環顧整個房間。他的視線落在一大塊紫色的布上。他拾起布，走到屏風後方。

「我討厭這幅畫。」他想。他露出一臉痛苦的表情，然後用那塊布蓋住了整幅畫。

接著，他帶著畫走上樓，走向舊書房。

「這個房間將守住我這一生的祕密。沒有人會在這裡看到這幅畫。我也不會看到它。我不想看著自己的靈魂在墮落。」他思忖著。

道林走出書房，再度將它上鎖。現在他覺得安心了。

P. 61

靈魂

• 回到 27 頁。道林說他的靈魂怎麼了？

• 道林的靈魂逐漸發生了什麼變化？當你在故事中看到「soul」這個字時，就把它劃底線作記號。

Chapter 8

P. 62

幾年過去了，道林仍然維持著他年輕姣好的面貌。不時，他生活方式的奇怪傳聞在倫敦流傳著。然而，他的外表看起來是如此無邪，說他有什麼惡行的事，都沒有人會相信。

他常常溜上樓，來到那個上鎖的房間，拿著鏡子，站在畫像前。他看著畫布裡邪惡變老的面容，然後又看看鏡中自己英俊年輕的臉龐，這個對比讓他很開心。他迷戀自己的美貌，也覺得自己靈魂的墮落感興趣。

春去秋來，花園裡花開花謝了好幾回，而道林一點都沒有改變。

後來發生了一件事。那是在十一月九號，就在道林三十八歲生日的前夕夜裡，約莫十一點的時候，道林走在回家的路上，霧中有一個人與他擦身而過。道林認出了那人，那是貝佐·哈霍。道林一陣莫名的恐懼向他襲來，他沒有打招呼，繼續邁步，但貝佐認出了他。

「道林！真幸運啊！我才剛從你家出來。我要搭午夜的火車到巴黎，在離開之前，我想見見你。你沒認出我來嗎？」

P. 63

道林回答：「我在霧中沒認出你，我連我的房子都認不出來了。很遺憾你要離開了，你很快就會回來嗎？」

「不會，我要去六個月。我想在巴黎弄個畫室。我們已經到你家門口了，讓我進去坐一會兒，我有話想跟你說。」

「好啦，但是你不會趕不上火車嗎？」道林走上門階開門時問道。

「我還有很多時間，火車十二點十五分才會發車，現在才十一點。」他回答。

道林看著他，笑笑地說道：「進來吧。」

貝佐跟著他走進了書房。

「現在我要跟你談正經事。」貝佐說。

「你要跟我談什麼？希望不是談我的事。」道林說。

「就是談你的事。外面的人把你講得很糟糕。」貝佐回答。

「我並不想知道。」

「但是道林，你不想人們説你壞話吧。當然，我是不相信你的那些流言。罪惡是寫在臉上的，掩藏不住。而你有一張青春無邪的臉，我無法相信任何詆毀你的話。他們説你帶壞了所有的朋友。」

P.64

「別説了，貝佐。」道林・格雷説。

「我要説，你也一定要聽。我想知道，我真的認識你嗎？在我回答得出來之前，我要先看看你的靈魂。」

「看我的靈魂！」道林・格雷嚇得臉色慘白。

「對，我要看看你的靈魂，但這只有上帝才做得到。」貝佐回答。

道林唇間迸出一聲苦笑。「跟我來，我讓你看看我的靈魂。那也是你的傑作。」

貝佐往後退了一步。

道林笑了。他從桌上取了蠟燭，平靜地説，「貝佐，上樓吧。我有寫生活日記，我讓你好好瞧瞧。」

「好吧，道林，我會過來看的，但是今晚不要叫我讀什麼東西。我要的，不過是簡單的回答我的問題。」

「你上樓就會找到答案，而且也不用讀什麼東西。」

Chapter 9

P.65

道林・格雷步走出房間，開始上樓，貝佐・哈霍跟在後面，燭光在牆上投出影子。當他們來到最上面時，道林打開門鎖。

「貝佐，你還是想看嗎？」他問。

「我想看。」貝佐説。

「很好。」他笑著答道。接著又説：「你是世上唯一應該知道我所有底細的人。你對我這一生的影響，超乎你的想像。」

這時他打開門，走了進去。

「進來後把門帶上。」他低聲説道。

貝佐帶著困惑的表情，環顧了道林的四周。整個房間滿布灰塵，有一股濕氣味。

「貝佐，你以為看得到靈魂的只有上帝嗎？把那塊布掀開，你就可以看到我的靈魂了。」道林以一種冷漠無情的聲音説。

「你瘋了，道林。」貝佐説。

「你不掀開那塊布，那我就自己來。」道林説罷，便把布簾拉到了地上。

當貝佐看到畫布上那張可怕的臉時，一聲驚恐的尖叫從他口中迸出。

P.67

天啊！那是道林・格雷的臉！在逐漸稀少的頭髮中，還看得到幾許金色，而眼眸仍是美麗的藍色。沒錯，那是道林，但是誰畫？看來像是出自於他的畫筆。

貝佐抓住蠟燭，舉到畫像旁邊，左下角寫著他的名字，長長的紅色字，是他

的畫沒錯。他不寒而慄。

他轉頭看著道林・格雷，喊道：「這是怎麼回事？」

「多年前，當我還是個年輕小伙子時，你恭維我，讓我開始虛榮。有一天，你介紹我認識你的一個朋友，他跟我說了青春的重要性。然後你的畫作完成了，我見識到了美的奇蹟，就在那個狂熱的時刻，我許了一個願……」道林・格雷說。

「我記得你的願望，但這是不可能的呀！這個房間濕氣重，會破壞畫布，顏料中也可能含有毒性的礦物成分。畫是不會變的，不可能會變的，你還跟我說過你已經把這幅畫毀了。」

「我說錯了，是它毀了我。」道林說。

「我不相信這是我的畫。我的肖像畫裡面不會有邪惡的成份。這是惡魔的臉孔。」

「這是我靈魂的臉孔。」

「它有惡魔的眼神。」

「貝佐，我們每個人的身上都有天堂和地獄。」道林大聲地說道。

P. 68

貝佐又轉身盯著那幅畫。

「天啊！如果這是真的，你一定比人們說的還惡劣！」貝佐叫喊道。

他又舉起燭火，端詳那幅畫。外觀看來是一樣的，那股邪惡是從內在透出來的，罪孽慢慢地蠶食了這幅畫。

他的手顫抖起來，蠟燭掉到了地板上，他於是用腳把燭火踩熄。他可以聽到道林在窗邊啜泣著。

天堂與地獄

- 道林說：「我們每個人的身上都有天堂和地獄。」你同意嗎？和夥伴討論。

「道林，禱告吧。」貝佐說。

道林・格雷緩慢地轉過身來，喊道：「太遲了，貝佐。」

「永遠不會太遲，道林。我們一起祈禱。」

道林看著那幅畫，突然對貝佐・哈霍生起一股恨意。畫布上的肖像在他耳邊低語著。他狂亂地環顧房間四周，瞥見到一把刀，那是他之前拿進來舊書房的。他緩緩朝著刀子移動，將刀子拿起。

P. 69

接著，他衝向貝佐，向他刺過去，一聲大叫迸出。道林不斷刺向貝佐。

他等了一會兒，然後把刀子丟在桌上。整個房子安靜了下來，沒有聲響，只有地板上流淌的血滴。

「我竟然這麼快就把他解決了！」他想。

道林感到異常的冷靜。他沒瞧那個被他殺掉的人，逕自走出房間，將身後的門鎖上，然後無聲無息地走下樓。

他來到書房，取出手錶，時間是一點四十分。

P. 70

他坐下來，開始思索。有沒有什麼不利於他的證據？「貝佐十一點時離開這裡，沒有人看到他再進來。我的男僕已經就寢了……巴黎！對，貝佐搭午夜的火車去巴黎了。」他想。

道林穿上毛草大衣，戴上帽子，步出屋外。接著他按了門鈴，五分鐘左右之後，男僕法蘭西斯出現了。

「很抱歉把你吵醒，法蘭西斯，但我忘了帶鑰匙了。現在幾點了？」他說。

「兩點十分，先生。」男僕回答。

「兩點十分了？這麼晚了！你明天九點一定要叫我起床，我有些事情要處理。」

「好的，先生。」

「今天晚上有人來訪嗎？」

「先生，哈霍先生有來。他待到十一點才走，要去趕火車。」

「可惜沒碰到他。他有留話嗎？」

「沒有，先生。他會從巴黎寫信給您。」

「謝謝你，法蘭西斯。晚安了。」

道林‧格雷把他的帽子和大衣丟在桌上，走進了書房。

有一刻鐘的時間，他在房裡來回踱步思考。接著，他從一個架上拿下通訊錄，開始翻頁。

「亞倫‧坎貝爾，梅費爾區，哈特佛街152 號。」

對，這就是他要的人。

Chapter 10

P. 71

　　隔天早上九點，男僕端著一杯巧克力進來，把窗簾拉開。十一月淡弱的陽光照進屋內。道林開始慢慢地想起昨天晚上發生的可怕事情。他對貝佐・哈霍仍懷有恨意。

　　「是他逼我殺他的。」他想。

　　現在屍體還在那兒，真可怕！他一定不要去想這件事。

　　他很快地起床換好衣服。他早餐吃了很久，然後坐在寫字桌前寫了兩封信，然後一封放進自己的口袋，一封交給了男僕。

　　「法蘭西斯，把這封信送去給哈特佛街152 號的坎貝爾先生。」

　　「如果亞倫・坎貝爾不在英格蘭，接下來我該怎麼辦？」他思忖著。

　　他們以前是很好的朋友，但現在兩個人碰面時，卻只有道林・格雷笑得出來，亞倫・坎貝爾都沒有笑容。

　　坎貝爾是個青年才俊。他熱愛科學，擁有自己的實驗室。他們兩個人都喜愛音樂，也會一塊兒去看歌劇和聽音樂會。

P. 72

　　他們的友誼持續了十八個月，後來兩個人突然不再來往，人們傳著流言流語。宴會上如果來了道林・格雷，亞倫・坎貝爾就會提早離席。坎貝爾變成一個人，他神情憂傷，而且不再彈鋼琴。這就是道林・格雷正在等候的人。道林時刻盯著時鐘，他很焦急，雙手發冷。

　　終於，亞倫・坎貝爾到了。他神情嚴峻，臉色發白。

　　「亞倫，你人真好，謝謝你來。」道林說。

　　「格雷，我不想再進你家了，但你說這件事攸關生死。」他的語氣生硬而冷淡的。

　　「沒錯，亞倫，坐下吧。」

　　坎貝爾拉了一張椅子到桌邊，道林坐在他對面。「亞倫，房子頂樓有一個上鎖的房間，裡面有一個死人，他現在已經死了十個小時了……」

　　「格雷，別說了，我不想要知道任何事情，把你的可怕祕密留給你自己吧。」

　　「亞倫，你可以救我。你懂化學，會做奇怪的實驗，你一定要銷毀樓上的屍體。沒有人看到這個人進房子，大家都以為他在巴黎。亞倫，你一定把他化為灰燼。」

　　「你瘋了，道林。我不會幫你。」

P. 73

　　「亞倫，這是謀殺，我殺了他。」道林說。

　　「謀殺！天啊，道林，你現在成了殺人犯了？」

　　「我只是要你銷毀屍體，這個屍體是唯一不利於我的證據。拜託，幫我，我們曾經是朋友。亞倫，他們會逮捕我！難道你不懂嗎？」

　　「我不幫。」

　　「你不幫？」

　　「沒錯。」

　　道林・格雷的眼裡流露出哀傷的神情。他拿了一張紙，在上面寫了寫，反覆讀了兩次，然後遞給坎貝爾。

坎貝爾一看，臉色發白。

「很抱歉，亞倫，我走投無路了。我已經寫了封信，就在這裡，你看看地址。如果你不幫我，我就把它寄出去。你現在無法拒絕了吧。」道林說。

亞倫遲疑了一下，「樓上的房間裡有火嗎？」

「有。」道林答道。

「我得回家從實驗室拿些東西來。」

「不，亞倫，你不可以離開這棟房子。我的僕人會搭馬車到你家，幫你拿那些東西來。」

這兩個人沉默地等著僕人回來。時鐘上的時間滴答滴答地緩慢流逝著。

P. 74

終於，門上傳來了敲門聲，僕人進到屋內。他拿著一大盒的化學藥品、一些金屬線，還有兩支鐵鉗。

「我要把這些東西放在這兒嗎，先生？」他問坎貝爾。

「對。」坎貝爾說。然後僕人就離開房間了。

「亞倫，我們現在要快點行動，跟我上樓。」道林說。

道林打開房門的鎖，一臉驚怖，說道：「亞倫，我想我沒辦法進去。」

「我不需要你。」坎貝爾冷漠地說。

P. 75

道林將門半掩，他看到自己畫像上那張可怕的臉，畫像前方的地板上，攤著那塊紫色的布。

「我忘記把那幅恐怖的畫藏起來了，我現在得把它蓋起來。」他想。

這時，他看到一隻手上有一滴紅血，太駭人了。他快步走進房間後，拿起那塊布，把布扔在畫上。

坎貝爾把那個沉重的箱子和鉗子拿進來。

「現在我自己來就好。」坎貝爾說。

道林轉身衝出房間。坎貝爾看著貝佐·哈霍死去的臉。道林在下樓時，聽到了坎貝爾鎖上房門的聲音。

坎貝爾回到書房時，已經過了七點。他臉色蒼白，但心情鎮定。

「我弄好了，就此再見了，我再也不想見到你了。」坎貝爾說。

「亞倫你，救了我一命，我不會忘記的。」道林說。

坎貝爾離開後，道林走上樓。房間裡有一股難聞的硝酸味，而屍體已經不見了。

生命

- 你認為道林的命值得救嗎？分組討論一下。

Chapter 11

P. 77

　　夜半時分，道林‧格雷悄悄溜出屋子。冰冷的雨落下來，起了濃霧。道林‧格雷搭了馬車，來到碼頭邊的小酒館。

　　「一個無辜的人死了，無可原諒。雖然寬恕是不可能，但是好歹可以遺忘。」他心想。

　　在小酒館的一個角落裡，坐著一位船員，他把頭埋在手臂裡趴在桌上。吧檯旁，站著兩位面容憔悴的婦人。

　　當他一進來，兩個畫著口紅的婦人，其中一個大聲的笑出來。

　　「惡魔來了！」她說。

　　「不要這樣叫我。」道林說，他決定起身離開。

　　「你希望大家叫你白馬王子，是嗎？」她在他身後大喊道。

　　她說話時，坐在桌邊的船員突然跳起來，他環顧四周，聽見酒館門閂上的聲音，便跑了出去。

　　道林‧格雷在雨中沿著碼頭快步走著，突然間，他感覺有隻手搭在了他的肩上，把他壓到了牆邊，接著一隻手圈住他的脖子，他掙扎求生。這時他聽到槍的喀擦聲，有支槍正抵住他的腦袋。

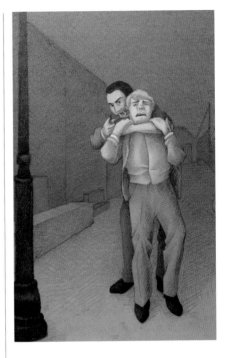

P. 79

　　「你要幹嘛？」道林大喊。

　　「安靜，你要是敢動，我就開槍。」那人說。

　　「你瘋了，我哪裡惹了你？」

船員

- 你想這個男子是誰？

　　「你毀了希貝兒‧魏恩的一生，希貝兒‧魏恩是我姊姊。」那人回答：「她自殺了，她的死都是你的錯，現在我要斃了你。我找了你好多年，沒找到。我只知道你的暱稱，今晚我聽到了，『白馬王子』」。

135

道林·格雷嚇得一陣噁心，「我沒聽過這個人，你瘋了。」他說。

「跪下！」那人大叫：「我的船今晚就要開往印度了，我要先宰了你。」

道林很驚恐，不知所措。突然，他有了一個想法。

「住手，你姊姊什麼時候死的？快，告訴我！」他大喊。

「十八年前，你問這個幹嘛？」那人說。

P. 80

「十八年前！」道林·格雷大笑說：「但你看看我的臉！」。

詹姆士·魏恩遲疑了一下，之後他開始打量道林·格雷的臉。那是二十歲男孩的臉。

「我航海到澳洲時，他只比我姊姊大一點點，這個人不可能是毀掉我姊一生的人。」他想。

他往後退了一步。

「天啊，我差點殺了你！」他大叫。

道林·格雷鬆了一口氣，「這是給你的警惕，不要親手報仇。」

「原諒我，先生，我錯了。」詹姆士·魏恩說。

「回家去，把槍收起來。」道林說罷，便轉身緩步沿著街道離開。

詹姆士·魏恩驚恐地望著他，全身從頭到腳顫抖著。

過了一會兒，一個黑色的身影來到燈下，朝他靠近。他感覺有隻手搭在他的手臂上，他回頭望，是酒吧裡那兩個女人當中的一位。

「你為什麼不殺了他？你這笨蛋！他有的是錢，但人很壞。」

「他不是我要找的人。錢我沒興趣，我要的那個人的命。我要找的人現在應該四十歲左右。這個人太年輕了。」詹姆士回答。

P. 81

這女人苦澀的笑了笑。「年輕！」她用不屑的口氣說：「我上回碰見白馬王子，是快十八年前的事了。」

「你胡說！」詹姆士·魏恩大喊。

「我說的是實話，傳說他為了那張漂亮的臉，把自己賣給了魔鬼。」她大聲地回話。「這十八年來他一點都沒變。」她補充道。

「真的？」

「對，是真的，但是不要跟他說，我怕他。」她喊道。

詹姆士·魏恩跑到街道的轉角處，但是已經不見道林·格雷了。

報仇

- 詹姆士·魏恩承諾過要對白馬王子做什麼？翻回第 41 和 42 頁去看看。

Chapter 12

P. 82

一個星期後，道林‧格雷在他鄉間的房子和一群朋友聚會。他們正在吃晚餐。道林嘻嘻笑笑，但不時感到害怕。突然間他環顧周圍，竟看見詹姆士‧魏恩的臉出現在窗戶外。道林‧格雷跳開眼神，當他再往回看時，那張臉就不見了。

「大概是我幻想出來，僕人並沒有來報告房子附近有陌生人，只是我自己的幻覺。希貝兒‧魏恩的弟弟並沒有回來殺我，他跟著他的船走了。我是安全的。」他心想。

隔天，道林開車穿過公園，去參加一場射擊會。

霧氣像一層鹽似的，灑在草地上，天空一片湛藍。在樹林的轉角處，他看見朋友傑佛瑞爵士拿著槍，他朝他走過去，想要加入他，這時突然一隻野兔從後面的灌木叢中衝出來。

傑佛瑞爵士把槍舉到肩上，但是道林‧格雷對那隻野兔有好感。

「別殺牠，傑佛瑞。」他大叫。

傑佛瑞爵士笑了笑。等野兔跳進灌木叢時，他才開了槍。他們聽到兩聲哀叫，一聲是野兔痛苦的哀號聲，另一聲是一個極度痛苦的男人的聲音。

P. 84

「老天啊！我射到人了！」傑佛瑞爵士驚恐的大叫。「別開槍！」他扯著喉嚨用力喊：「有人受傷了。」

獵場管理員跑過來，喊道：「在哪裡？他在哪裡？」

「在這裡。」傑佛瑞爵士朝灌木叢跑去，氣呼呼地說道。

道林看著他們。幾分鐘後，他們拖著一個人走了出來。他害怕地轉過身。

「人死了嗎？」傑佛瑞爵士問。

「死了。」獵場管理員回答。

幾分鐘後，道林感覺有隻手搭在他的肩膀上，他轉過身。

「道林，走，我們回去了。」亨利勳爵說。

他們肩並肩走著，不發一語。

這時，道林看著亨利勳爵，嘆口氣道：「亨利，這是個凶兆，有恐怖的事情就要發生在我身上了。」

長者笑了笑，「道林，到底能有什麼事發生？」

「別這樣笑。我想逃離這裡，我會叫哈維把遊艇準備好，到了遊艇上，我就沒事了。」

「道林，你是要從什麼事裡抽身？你惹了什麼禍？跟我講，你知道我會幫你。」

「我不能告訴你，亨利。我現在要去躺一下，我累了。」道林哀傷的回答說。

惹禍

- 當你惹禍時，你會想要告訴誰？
- 你覺得找人講，能幫得上忙嗎？跟朋友討論一下。

道林在房裡休息時，獵場管理員來找他。

「桑頓，你是為了早上的意外而來的嗎？」道林問。

「是的，先生」獵場管理員說。

「那個可憐的人有妻小嗎？我想送點錢過去。」道林問他。

「我們不知道他的身分，他看起來像是個船員。」

「船員？你是說船員？」道林大喊。

「是的，他兩隻手臂上都有刺青。」

道林站起身來，問道：「屍體在哪裡？快！我要立刻去看看。」

「在荷姆農莊的空馬廄裡，先生。」

P. 86

「荷姆農莊！現在馬上就去，我跟著你走。」

不到一刻鐘的時間，道林·格雷就騎著馬飛奔在這長路上，一路上石子飛揚，最後終於抵達了荷姆農莊。

其中一個馬廄亮著燈。他急忙走到門邊，準備開門。這時他遲疑了一下，眼前這一刻就要決定他人生的成敗了。

接著，他打開門，走了進去。死者躺在遠遠的角落裡，臉上蓋了一條斑點手帕。道林·格雷叫了一名農莊的奴僕過來。

「把他臉上的手帕拿起來，我要看看。」他說。

農莊奴僕把手帕拿起來，道林·格雷高興地哭了出來。

這個人是詹姆士·魏恩。

道林站在那裡看著屍體好一會兒。

他在騎馬回家的路上，眼裡滿了淚水，因為他知道他沒事了。

Chapter 13

P. 87

幾個星期之後，道林去拜訪亨利勳爵。

「不要跟我說你想要變好，你已經很完美了，不需要改變。」亨利勳爵大聲說。

道林·格雷搖搖頭，「我這一生做了太多可怕的事，我要金盆洗手了。別說我的事了。最近城裡有什麼事嗎？我好幾天沒去俱樂部了。」

「人們還是在講貝佐失蹤的事。」

「我以為大家已經對那個話題膩了。」道林說。

「親愛的孩子，這件事也才講了六個星期。大家這陣子很幸運，茶餘飯後有我的離婚和亞倫·坎貝爾的自殺可以聊。」

「你想貝佐是怎麼了？」道林沉著地問。

「不知道。」

「要是我說貝佐被我殺了呢？」

「你不可能殺人的，道林。別說貝佐的事了，他搞不好是從巴士上摔進塞納河

138

裡了。對了，他替你畫的那幅很俊美的肖像在哪裡？喔，我現在想起來了！幾年前，你跟我說過，你把畫送去賽爾拜莊園，結果在途中弄丟了還是被偷了。真可惜啊，我本來還想買下它的，真希望它現在就在我手上。」

「我一直就不是真的喜歡它。」道林說。

P. 89

「道林，你是怎麼保持年輕的？你一定有祕方。我只比你大十歲，但是我已經滿臉皺紋、老態龍鍾了。拜託，告訴我你的祕方。為了要找回我的青春，除了運動、早起、維持好名聲，什麼事我都願意做。」

亨利勳爵

• 在找回青春這件事上，亨利勳爵不想做些什麼？

當天晚上，道林返回家中後，便打發僕人就寢，然後自己坐在書房的沙發上，接著他開始回想自己的人生。

「我帶壞我的朋友，毀了很多青年才俊的一生。啊，我何苦祈求讓肖像變老、讓自己永保青春？我想要美貌與永恆的青春，但它們卻毀了我。往事不堪回首，逝者難追，我要往前看。詹姆士・魏恩死了，亞倫・坎貝爾也死了。他半夜裡在他自己的實驗室舉槍自殺了。」他想。

他繼續思忖，「我現在沒事了。貝佐畫了那幅毀了我人生的肖畫，在這件事情上我無法原諒他。一切都是那幅畫像的錯。」

P. 91

他開始思索那幅肖畫。

「要是我變好了，搞不好那幅畫像就可能再變美。我要去瞧瞧。」他想。

他拿起桌上的燈，走上樓去。當他打開門鎖時，他笑了。

「是的，我會變好，我不用再害怕這幅畫了。」他想。

他上樓，走進房間，鎖上門。接著，他拉掉畫像上的紫色布，發出了一聲痛苦的叫聲。

畫像變得更恐怖了，臉看起來更邪惡了，手上和腳上也都出現了新的血跡。

・道林會變好嗎？或是為時已晚了？

道林嚇得打哆嗦。

「我要供認我殺了貝佐嗎？不，這是個愚蠢的想法。現在只有一個不利於我的證據，那就是這幅畫。我要毀了它，我幹嘛把它留了這麼久？當然，它一直是我的良心寫照，但是我現在要把它毀了。」他想。

P.92

畫像

・在 52 頁中，道林發現他的畫像就是他的良心，而他現在想把它毀了。你認為人的良心有可能被毀掉嗎？分組討論一下。

道林環顧房間，看到了自己刺殺貝佐・哈霍的那把刀。刀子正閃閃發亮著。

「這把刀殺了畫家，現在這把刀也要用來銷毀畫家的作品。過去的事就要被銷毀了，等它銷毀了，我就自由了。」他想。

他抓起那把刀，刺向畫像，這時傳出叫喊聲和摔落聲。叫喊聲如此淒厲，吵醒了僕人們，他們從各自的房間跑出來，不知如何是好。老管家黎夫太太開始哭出來。

大約一刻鐘後，法蘭西斯找了另外兩個佣人一起上樓。他們敲了房門，但沒有回應。他們又大聲叫喊，還是沒有人應聲。他們開不了門。最後，他們爬上屋頂，往下跳到書房的陽臺上。窗戶的鎖很老舊，一下子就打開了。

P.94

他們進去房間，看到一幅道林・格雷年輕時的美麗肖像畫，畫像前方的地板上，倒臥著一個死去的男人。

倒在地板上的男人，一臉皺紋，上了年紀，而且有一張邪氣的臉。

一直到他們看到了戒指，才認出了那個人是誰。

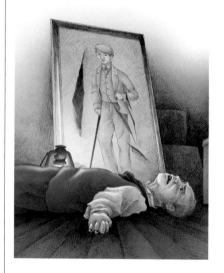

Before Reading

1 1. b 2. d 3. c 4. a 5. e 6. f
2 1. a 2. c 3. b 4. d

4 1. b 2. d 3. e 4. c 5. f 6. a
5 a) 4 b) 7 c) 6 d) 1 e) 3 f) 10
g) 9 h) 5 i) 2 j) 8
6 a) mysterious
b) Laughter
c) Youth
d) tired, curious, disappointed

8 b)
9 a death, a murder, a romance
10 a) romance
b) horror

After Reading

6 a) F b) T c) T d) F e) T f) F
7 a) 5 b) 3 c) 1 d) 6 e) 4 f) 2 g) 8 h) 7

8 a) 2 b) 3 c) 5 d) 4 e) 6 f) 1
10 vain, selfish, cruel, charming, attractive
11 a) kind
b) selfish
c) young
d) old
e) good-looking
f) evil
g) ugly

13 a) Sibyl Vane
b) Dorian Gray
c) Basil Hallward
d) Dorian Gray
e) James Vane
f) Basil Hallward
14 a) conscience
b) life
c) change
d) cruelty
e) good
f) evil (x2)
* Basil says c) and f).
15 Sentence C is untrue.
16 a) 2 b) 1 c) 3

17 a) T b) T c) F d) T e) F f) T g) F
18 b)
20 a) 3 b) 4 c) 6 d) 1 e) 2 f) 5
21 a) hideous
b) confident
c) fascinated
d) miserable
e) extraordinary
f) terrible

22 a) portraits
b) gun
c) poison
d) theater
23 a) 4 b) 6 c) 5 d) 1 e) 8 f) 3 g) 2 h) 7
24 a) was painted
b) shot
c) were destroyed
d) committed
e) was (never) exhibited
f) was murdered
g) stabbed

Test

Pages 106-107

1 a) 3 b) 2 c) 4 d) 2 e) 4

2
   a) Dorian Gray is very good-looking.
      He has got golden hair, fair skin, blue
      eyes and red lips.
   b) The painting shows the secret of his
      soul. There is too much of himself in
      the painting.
   c) He wishes that the portrait could
      grow old and he could stay young.
   d) He thinks Lord Henry will be a bad
      influence on Dorian.
   e) Dorian can play the piano.
   f) He falls in love with a beautiful young
      actress, Sibyl Vane.
   g) He first notices a change after he tells
      Sibyl that he never wants to see her
      again.
   h) He hides the portrait behind a screen.
   i) He puts the portrait in the old
      schoolroom where nobody can see it.
   j) He shows it to Basil Hallward. He asks
      to see Dorian's soul.
   k) James Vane tries to kill Dorian.
   l) Dorian tells James Vane that he is too
      young to be the man Sibyl fell in love
      with. James Vane believes him.
   m) Dorian Gray murders Basil Hallward.
      Sibyl Vane and Alan Campbell commit
      suicide. Sir Geoffrey shoots James
      Vane by mistake.
   n) Dorian Gray kills himself when he tries
      to destroy the portrait.
   o) The portrait becomes young and
      good-looking again.

國家圖書館出版品預行編目資料

道林‧格雷的畫像 / Oscar Wilde 著；
林育珊 譯. 一初版. 一[臺北市]：寂天文化,
2015.12 面；公分. 中英對照

ISBN 978-986-318-406-5 (平裝附光碟片)
1. 英語 2. 讀本

805.18   104024589

原著 _ Oscar Wilde
改寫 _ Elspeth Rawstron
譯者 _ 林育珊
校對 _ 陳慧莉
製程管理 _ 洪巧玲
出版者 _ 寂天文化事業股份有限公司
電話 _ +886-2-2365-9739
傳真 _ +886-2-2365-9835
網址 _ www.icosmos.com.tw
讀者服務 _ onlineservice@icosmos.com.tw
出版日期 _ 2015年12月 初版一刷（250101）
郵撥帳號 _ 1998620-0 寂天文化事業股份有限公司